The Case of the

Criminal Walk

and Other Stories

Hama Tuma

Outskirts Press, Inc.
Denver, Colorado

Outskirts Press
http://www.outskirtspress.com

ISBN-10: 1-59800-367-4
ISBN-13: 978-1-59800-367-3

Dedication

The arrogance of power is still there, injustice abounds but the martyrs and silent and discreet heroes are remembered and their banner still flies high under the Ethiopian sky.

This one is dedicated to two heroes of different molds: to my late brother and comrade Samuel Alemayehu who gave me the support to continue writing and to the late Poet Laureate Tsegaye Gebre Medhin whom I called a friend.

It is also dedicated to the real Captain Berhanu and to Colonel Solomon, two of a kind who traveled the distance with courage. And finally to Manyazewal, who not only devoured books but committed to memory entire chapters, the real Matteos, who would have enjoyed the stories and countered with more.

Table of Contents

Prologue   1

The Other Son   7

The Anderibi Story   43

The Case Of The Criminal Walk   57

The Coward Who Hid His Eyes   69

The Woman With A Grievance   96

The Garbage Baby   108

The Mob   118

The Rumors Bar   122

Of Dreams And Death   134

The Man With Another Face   138

The Trip Within   143

The Sheratonians   148

Epilogue   171

Prologue

It was a City founded by an Emperor for his wife who, legend has it, wanted her husband to settle down, to put an end to roving capitals of tents pitched here and there, a nomadic existence, a test on monogamy. It had started out as a series of scattered villages at an altitude of 2400 meters dominated by a mountain and several hills, with the Emperor's palace on top of the largest hill. Since then, many more palaces have been built and have been forced to welcome new occupants.

Captain Berhanu was born in the City, somewhere on the Street named for the patriots who had fought against the Italian invaders, as you drive up the Gulele. He finished primary and secondary schooling here, tasted sex with his first girl up in the Yakob forest, joined the Police College, graduated, witnessed some marriages and many deaths, saw friends turn enemies and brave people into cowards. On this particular sunny morning as he carefully drove his battered Volkswagen to his office through narrow back streets packed with pedestrians and loaded donkeys, his mind was back to his younger days and to the captivating smell of eucalyptus, roasting coffee, spices and burning cow dung that, in his mind, would always characterize his City.

Nowadays, the sprawling City, home to some four million souls (of whom many hundreds of thousands slept in the streets or had no real homes), did not live up to the New Flower name that had been given it by an optimist Empress on its foundation. Sprawl it had instead of bloom, but Captain Berhanu did not forget that in the prevalent misery that tried to choke all signs of hope and joy, there were the resolute people with tight and haggard faces who refused to give up. The City had seen far too many deaths, at least three massacres (one by an Italian invading force, two by local rulers), but it had survived. It was, at least for Captain Berhanu, alive.

Back in its early days, you could see in the City barefooted soldiers with bolt rifles, nobles on mule backs with their armed servants running alongside them, dogs roving the unpaved streets during the day and hyenas coming down from the hills to scavenge at night. Beggars were aplenty then also but never reaching the numbers they have now. Back then you could see a corpse or two hanging from a tree or a scaffold, a sight that continued even during the last Emperor's time, to be replaced by hundreds of mutilated corpses being exposed on the streets as a cruel military dictator tried to stamp out opposition through a terror that it labeled Red. There were then as now the open markets, the 'gulits', men and women squatting in front of their varied wares. Nowadays you will not see a debtor and a creditor chained together or a convicted person being flogged in public but the caravan of loaded donkeys, the convoy of bent women carrying firewood, drunks staggering up the roads, and the cruel punishments are still there.

The City had changed and yet remained the same like the life of the people. It now has more prostitutes and bars and brothels. There was in the past only the Wube Berha (or the Desert as the city folk with some knowledge of English called it) to serve as the red light district. Then came the Nefas Silk and before you could say enough every corner of the City had its bars and brothels for all classes. Multi-storied buildings vied for space with ram shackled tin roofed houses, cars of different makes and values clogged the often pot-holed streets, donkeys and humans crowded the sidewalks, few men now wore the traditional Shamma, there are more churches and mosques competitively shouting their calls to the faithful via microphones. There is no longer an European Quarter as in the old days but there are the posh districts of walled villas where the depraved passions and greed of the ruling elite flourish, away from the public eye. There is more dirt and filth nowadays but the hot springs of the Filowha are still there for those who can afford it. You can still drink local araq, tella and tej but changing times have brought in different types of beer, whiskey, and cognac. More people smoked cigarettes than in the past, the "itsefaris" that only priests were supposed to take has been replaced by modern and more damaging drugs. If in the past only Moslem traders and students from Harar or Dire Dawa chewed Kat, nowadays almost every City dweller, young or old, spent money and time chewing on the mildly hallucinogenic leaves every day. Kat parlors were all over the City, motels and hotels at every corner, preteen girls, many carrying the deadly virus, walked up and down the streets looking for customers. The main railway station, the Legehar as it became known modifying the French's name for it, La Gare, was still there, unchanged, a sign of an Emperor's foresight and a foreign power's dubious interest in the region and a testimony to the dilapidation that has gripped the City.

There was a famous patriot, Dejazmatch Takele, who wanted to burn the whole City down frustrated by the inhabitants' reluctance to join the patriots battling against the occupying soldiers of Mussolini, but fate had saved the City from being reduced to ashes. It was perhaps symbolic of the soul of the City, Captain Berhanu had wondered many times as he contemplated on what really defined the City he loved and, at times, also hated with passion. So many cemeteries all over the city held underground not only corpses but also very many dreams by those who had dared to have a vision but who had almost all perished. The famous patriot who had wanted to burn the City down and who was years later to die violently still struggling for change--few people remembered him now.

There was the General and his brother and officer friends who tried to stage a coup and were hanged, shot or committed suicide. There were the thousands of youngsters who dared to challenge a ruthless military regime and were consumed by the officially declared Red Terror. And the many others who were still seeing the dawn and stretching to seize it and being cut down by the dark forces of evil. For Captain Berhanu, the City was the sum of its dirt poor and indecently rich inhabitants, of their dreams and fears, their passions and yearnings, their hostilities and similarities as citizens of a country the tourist brochures describe as an old country "beyond all imaginings" and yet threatened by the fetid politics of what the continent called "tribalists".

Captain Berhanu knew that the City, which held all his memories and in which, as the saying goes, his umbilical cords are buried, this City and its people would survive the present cruel rulers too, not unscathed but wounded and alive. He knew like most that times have changed and made the test of one's worth much more difficult. As people say in disbelief, the children of the Nile were going thirsty. The glorious past and history of the people was being questioned, the pride that characterized the Nation scoffed at as "hualaqer", reactionary, or even as "timkhit", chauvinism. It seemed as if promises made but never kept no longer haunted, that words had become lighter than a swallow's feather, as if all the scribes have been bought by the powerful to chronicle the lies as sacred. The hyenas have long disappeared as yet another victim of the expansion of the City and what was called modernism, the eucalyptus trees have dwindled and the people, grappling with what is called modern seemed to have compromised their identity and heritage, their self respect and uniqueness. Districts were no longer called sefer but kebelles and yet they had not changed much.

Going against the odds, Captain Berhanu believed, that all was not lost. The daisies were still around, the jacarandas, mimosas and roses still abound, and beyond the sight of half naked street children and deformed beggars, above the stifling poverty and degradation of all sorts, and beyond the symphony of hate orchestrated by narrow minded rulers, the City was still alive, alive with its people, vibrant with a hope that refused to give up or die come what may. He had met with many cruelties in his line of work but he refused to be embittered and pessimistic about his City and people.

Captain Berhanu was just one of the children of the City. His was a life dedicated to serving others, "in my own way" as he often qualified it. Others in the City also lived what they were dealt out as life to the best they could. The wealthy patrons of the Sheraton Hotel who debated on the tastes of Belugia caviar and pate de foie gras imported from France and the hungry many who slept on the dirty streets huddled together for warmth, the thieves and muggers, the teachers and civil servants, the priests and monks, the sheikhs and muftis, the con artists and the whores, the child prostitutes and the drug pushers, the soldiers and the police, the displaced multitudes with empty stomachs and tattered cloths, of all ages and backgrounds and mother tongues-- they all called the City home. It was indeed the melting pot, the continuing symbol of people speaking different mother tongues and yet talked the same language and is one people. As people say, if one calls it a life, sleeping in a cemetery can be comfortable. The City dwellers were adept now at avoiding great expectations. There was much generosity in the City but it was also a man eat man world in there and therefore the motto was "have no goat and no tiger will stalk you". Yet, the poor knew that no one left them alone because they had little or nothing. They knew they still had their eyes, their memories and always posed as potential dangers to those in power, with the ill-gotten wealth. Aren't a people with memory and grievances like a sharpened knife kept inside its sheath, waiting for its time?

To each his own life and as one chronicler of the City's life wrote "who can say these days that the people live better than the stray dogs and overworked donkeys?"

Maybe no one can, but one can attempt to write about the people and their lives shaped by despair and death as well as hope and optimism. The stories in this collection are such tales of the City and its people. It is proper also that the first story should be that involving Captain Berhanu, son of the City he called home.

The Other Son

"She gauged out the boy's eyes and used him as a beggar. Good morning."

Captain Berhanu nodded at Lieutenant Solomon, with whom he shared an office, and finished hanging his coat on the nail on the wall behind his desk.

"Both eyes? Good morning to you too." Captain Berhanu sat down and started checking his morning files.

"Both eyes", Lt. Solomon confirmed. "He brought her forty to fifty every day."

"Birr or cents?" asked Captain Berhanu though he could guess the answer.

"Birr of course."

"I hardly knew that there were still people out there with the heart and the money to give alms to beggars."

It was a City of beggars--thousands and thousands of them. Uprooted, impoverished, war veterans, displaced, evicted by warlords driven by hate and ethnic politics, children orphaned by war or AIDS, the maimed and disfigured, famine victims, beggars of all ages and deformities and miseries stifled the City and poked at the tired hearts and empty pockets of the City folk. The rich and the heartless tried to keep within the sanitized confines of their four-wheel drives with tinted windows, their walled comfortable villas, some with the coveted swimming pools, and the plush drinking bars of the ultra-modern high class hotels like the Arab-built Sheraton which contrasted grotesquely with the slums besieging it and all posh villas.

"Can you draw blood from an ant? The rich do not give, they just have a better PR sense," said Lt. Solomon. "I suspect it is the poor who share out the little that they have. Distribution of poverty or structural adjustment Ethiopian style if you prefer."

"Still, forty to fifty is a big amount. And young blind beggars are not rare at all."

"The sergeant told me this particular blind boy looks angelic," explained Lt. Solomon. "He is able to draw sympathy from our hard hearted folks, a real gold mine for the boss-lady. The report says she lured him from a village and had him blinded in the Mercato."

The Mercato, the New Market. One of the biggest sprawling market places in Africa, the historic place had for long been a landmark of the city. It was now on the verge of being sold to any interested foreign buyer by a government that had little sense of history or pride. In the Mercato, you can buy spices as well as professional killers, you can shop for shoes and shirts or haggle with a man who rents out children to serve as beggars. You can hide from the police or buy a policeman's death. The Mercato smelt mixed, rotten and fresh, promising and stale, and was in the seventies the fief of an underground movement that had almost toppled the military government. Though the country's poet laureate had once penned a moving poem in its name, the Mercato has now become as faded as most of the country and the prospect of its being sold to foreigners was not even raising much feeling in its inhabitants.

"What do they want us to do with the case?"

"They shuffled it here for the formality," said Lt. Solomon.

"The usual routine. To say they do nothing behind our backs. Just stroking our egos. They have already released the woman."

"She hails from their place?"

"As coffee from Kaffa."

"They" were the new rulers of the country. Hard and cruel ethnic guerrillas who had made it to the Palace benefiting from the violent excesses of a ruthless military regime that slaughtered the more promising opposition and had left the field free for their hate- driven politics. Unpatriotic, and on sale for the highest bidder, they were avidly courted by the enemies of the country and had thus benefited from the backing of regional and international forces. They had put in place a one-ethnic based government that paid lip service to all the current clichés and buzz words of the so called Donor Countries while staffing the State bureaucracy and the key posts with the members of their own ethnic group from the north. "They" also controlled and run the Criminal Investigation Department (CID) as a whole and the Homicide Department for which Captain Berhanu and Lt. Solomon worked.

In fact, both had worked for the CID-Homicide section for more years than they cared to remember. Graduates of the former Abadina Police College, they had both shown an inclination to honesty and professional dedication to their work and immediately appeared as anomalies, as suspects, in a country where those in power considered honesty and integrity as dangerous naivety. Their apparent lack of zeal for the crude military rule in place at the time and their reluctance to join the bandwagon and the unique ruling Party like many of their colleagues who had, practically overnight, turned from Royalists to red-hot Marxist-Leninists, had earned them undeclared punishments. Both had been posted to remote and dangerous rural areas and forgotten, but both had survived. Captain Berhanu was recalled back to the City earlier than Lt. Solomon who was summoned just before the military regime collapsed. Of the two, who were long time friends sharing a common disdain for those in power, contempt for cowards, love for books and the cinema, and an aversion for a pompous African author who wrote of Kafka-quoting rural folks, Lt. Solomon was the outspoken one whose 'dare to reply' motto had earned him a demotion at least once.

"Forget the case then," said Captain Berhanu leafing through the morning file. "If they already released the woman there is nothing we can do. Is there really anything we can do anytime?"

They shared a small office already filled up by their two chairs and tables. At one corner there were two worn out and wobbly looking wooden chairs with an iron filing-box in between. A Spartan and cold room, it meshed with the prevailing detached and sour mood of the two friends.

"Here is a case fit for the tabloids," said Captain Berhanu. "Have you read of the strange man who shakes your hands and as he does so makes your penis disappear?"

Lt. Solomon burst out laughing. "Good riddance is what people should say in these days of the Scourge."

Captain Berhanu smiled and continued reading. "The case is brought to our attention because one alleged victim attempted to kill him and was apprehended. The victim alleges that the wizard, or "metetegna" as he calls the man, made his penis vanish and when he had paid him a hundred Birr made it reappear."

"What's his problem then?"

"He alleges that the wizard gave him a new penis, not black or brown, but that of an Albino".

"I wonder what that would look like," said Lt. Solomon. "And who cares anyways? Not many people I know make love with the lights on."

Captain Berhanu closed the file and threw it into the OUT tray. "Who cares indeed? The fellow still has a penis and he should be thankful. I m sure there are many women out there who would think an Albino penis has magical and medicinal values. To think we are reduced to this. Homicide, my foot! A country reeking of crimes and we deal with such junk!"

Captain Berhanu knew full well that such were the cases

they were mostly allowed to investigate even though they belonged to the Homicide section. The big criminals were almost all people in power, away from the prying eyes of any CID captain. Political murders were aplenty but they were investigated, or rather shelved aside, by the political police that was almost entirely made up of the members of the elite ethnic group. Where criminal cases involved in one way or another any member of the elite group, officers hailing from that region also handled the cases.

"Worse still," said Lt. Solomon breaking into the Captain's reverie. "I have been assigned specifically to follow the case of the morgue."

This, as Captain Berhanu was to find out, involved a criminal act which ensued after the relatives of a dead woman in the morgue alleged that a male corpse had arisen in the night and raped their dead kin and thereby fouled her and made her journey to heaven impossible. The relatives of the dead man did not dispute the fact that the man did have the power to resurrect, to rape a fellow corpse and then to become a corpse again but argued that such things are in the realm of miracles and involve only God. In short, they refused to pay compensation money and the expenses for the costly church rites to re-cleanse the woman's body. Following the refusal to pay, a relative of the woman had broken into the morgue, or so the accusation went, and chopped off the penis of the male corpse who had had the gall to rape the dead woman.

"Is there a penal code article to deal with such things?"

"Breaking and entry into a morgue is a crime," said Lt. Solomon. "Chopping off someone's penis even when he does not need it is another one. Rape is still a crime hard as it is to believe how it could be so when we see how the powerful bed underage girls everyday of the week."

"Well, at least you have some dead bodies to deal with," said captain Berhanu.

There came a knock at the door.

"Come in," invited Captain Berhanu..

A thin and tall man in a Corporal's uniform entered,

saluted the two officers and handed a file to the Captain. "A murder sir," he told the Captain. "The report just came in this morning."

"Where?" asked the Captain, opening the file. There was only a single sheet of paper in it.

"Gulele," said the Corporal. "The Abadinas have already gone in their van." Abadinas was the name that had been given to the scientific and technical team since almost all were graduates of the prestigious and now closed Abadina Police College. Captain Berhanu, who lived not far from the Gulele, just near the Arbegnotch Elementary School, nodded with a smile. Abadinas by God, he said to himself. The trained technicians had almost all been purged by the new government and replaced by amateurs who knew practically nothing about their supposed job but were given the post on ethnic grounds and considerations. Gulele or Yaya Gulele as some had tried to call it in a frenzy of name changing that was in vogue some years back, was fast becoming a hot crime area.

"Okay thanks," said Captain Berhanu and started reading aloud the one page report after the corporal left.

"This morning around 8.45 am, Ato Mulu Negew was found stabbed to death in his two room house in the Gulele, near the former Medhane Alem school (Kebelle, house no........) Fifty- six years old Ato Mulu lived alone, and his body was discovered by his sister who had come to visit him from the Kebena area. Ato Mulu was born of an Oromo father and an Amhara mother in Ambo town. During the previous regime, he was allegedly a Kebelle official and after the downfall of the military regime he was arrested for possible Red Terror crimes but released for lack of any proof or witnesses. Captain Berhanu is hereby assigned to the case and should report back as soon as possible."

There was an illegible signature the Captain knew belonged to his superior, a desk- man who had been catapulted from being a civilian to a colonel's post in the Criminal Investigation Department, non-uniformed or detectives' section, because his wife was related to some bigwig in the

Prime Minister's Office. The colonel treaded on safe grounds by never venturing to do anything. The brief report was also sanitized and consistent with the times by mentioning the ethnic origin of the deceased. Mulu Negew, what kind of man were you, Captain Berhanu pondered to himself as he put on his coat, wrote the Gulele address on a piece of paper, wished Lt. Solomon good luck with the rapist corpse and went to his battered Volkswagen car.

Sometimes, he felt it was as if all the inhabitants of the sprawling City had taken a vow to rot and to stink their own city. The stench was unbearable, a mixture of human excrement, rotting garbage piled high at every corner, the acid smell of sweating and unwashed bodies, of rancid butter women put on their hair, and of overflowing sewage pipes. He had learnt to ignore the stench and all that soiled the image of the City in his memory. He who had loved the city's smell of eucalyptus trees, roasting coffee and the smoke from the burning cow dung used as firewood had to learn to accommodate and live with the new stench of hopelessness and despair brought in by the new rulers to aggravate the overall decay. Near the St. Yohannes church, he saw so many amputees that he wondered if the machete-wielding child soldiers of Sierra Leone's Fode Sankoh had come to town. He had read an article that claimed foreigners were writing of the warmth of the people and the beauty of the City, but he who had loved his people had been of late incapable of seeing any exoticism in the heat and dirt, in the poverty and despair that had eaten into the very soul of the people and made them not only physically bent and haggard but had also turned most of them into unprincipled and tactical beings. Yet, he could not deny he loved the City and its people much as parents would love their newborn baby, with dirty diapers and all.

As he drove his creaking Volkswagen, he took care to avoid the mini- vans that served as taxis, locally called "Weyiyit", Matatu in Kenya and Boksi or Berentsa in the Sudan. The name Weyiyit, discussion, was given to the mini vans because the passengers sat facing each other but in actual fact little talk took place as everyone carried his or her fear along and open talk could lead to prison or worse if a spy (and they were many) happened to be around. He called the mini-vans the Grim Reaper's foot soldiers as they sped dangerously and in the congested streets where humans sane and insane, donkeys, and cars of all types competed for space, they usually caused fatal accidents. He had heard and half believed the exaggerated claim that most of the drivers and tout boys, called Weyalas, were University and High School drop- outs who could not get a better job. They allegedly took out their frustrations on the street and on the passengers they push and stuff in like sardines into the mini vans.

Captain Berhanu drove carefully and rather slowly. The streets were crowded and noisy and he was driving to the Gulele where preteen girls plied the roads as prostitutes. He saw elderly and young women their backs bent by heavy loads; sweat covering their haggard faces sucked dry of any sign of relief or joy. There were the "arambists", the usual semi-naked preteen boys their mouths and noses covered by rags soaked in petrol, their walk unsteady. The beggars were aplenty too. He saw a mother holding a child with an enormous head, down the street an elderly man was sitting with his swollen and deformed penis exposed, there were amputees, shriveled old men and women, many blind ones or those faking it. As usual, he was not struck by the kind and variety of the deformities but was once again affected by the new kind of beggars, normal people, young and old, without any physical deformity whatsoever, just bent and burdened by the shame of their conditions, stretching their hands ever hesitantly to beg. This, he considered, was an indication of the lowest depths to which the City and, along with it, the country had sunk. In the past, begging was an unbearable shame and tolerated only by and with those who were physically handicapped in one way or another. Nowadays, the State itself was an international beggar and everyone could beg and live with the shame.

It took him more than half an hour to reach the site of the crime. The house was in a compound, a tin roofed dwelling with a wooden fence that was in disrepair. Captain Berhanu knew that having one's own house in an enclosed compound was no ordinary thing, it indicated that, in this city where more than half the people could be safely declared homeless, the victim was no poor man living ten to twelve in a small compound of tiny kiosk-like rooms and shared outhouses. The policeman at the gate saluted him.

As he entered the house, he found himself in a small living room crowded by the members of the technical team. A sergeant from the CID, whom Captain Berhanu knew by name as Lemma, approached him.

"Good morning Captain," said the sergeant gesturing to the floor where the dead man lay in a pool of blood. "He had been stabbed several times in the chest and stomach as you can see. Sometime in the morning, says the doctor. The killer had chopped off the victim's penis and left it on his chest but we have removed it. His sister found him this morning. Nothing seems to have been robbed but we are checking on that too."

"Where is the sister now?" asked Captain Berhanu.

"Neighbors are taking care of her in the next compound."

"The murder weapon?"

"A knife for sure but we have not found it."

"Was the victim living alone?" As he asked this, Captain Berhanu stepped around the corpse and checked the two bookshelves near the table carrying a hi-fi set. Political books in English and Amharic, translations of Soviet era novels, Gorky mostly, thrillers by Archer, Ludlum and Grafton, books by Achebe, Mwangi, Ousmane, Ngugi, and Amharic classics ranging from Tobia and Araya to Fikr Iske Mekabir, a Bible in Oromiffa, the shelves were full and Captain Berhanu had no doubt that the dead man was a literate, and thereby a strange person in a country where the prime minister boasts of not "wasting his time on reading".

"Yes," replied sergeant Lemma.

"Any chance of these professionals getting a finger print?" asked Captain Berhanu with a smile.

"Most of it theirs," replied the sergeant, an elderly man

who had worked with the real Abadinas in the past. "As you can see, sir, they are not wearing any gloves."

Captain Berhanu knew the sergeant did not hail from the North and so dared to comment: "everything to the North and no cent for gloves". The Sergeant smiled knowingly.

"I will talk to the sister," said Captain Berhanu. "Supervise the team here and make sure the body goes to the Morgue. And get me detailed report of the post mortem. Which side is the neighbor's house?"

Having been told that the neighbors sheltering the sister were in the next compound on the right Captain Berhanu made his way there. The gate was open and he went in without knocking. The house had a verandah with two wooden chairs and a rickety table. He knocked at the door and an elderly man opened it.

"Good morning. I am Captain Berhanu from the CID. I will like to talk to the sister of the man who died next door."

"Come in," said the elderly man and Captain Berhanu was ushered into the small living room that smelt of incense and of the red pepper and garlic usually used to cook the traditional sauces. A middle-aged woman sat on one sofa chair weeping while an older woman at her side was pleading with her to stop weeping.

"Please sit down," the host invited pointing at a sofa chair. "We have been telling her to stop crying herself to death. We live in terrible times, don't we? Thousands of the young die every day. Useless deaths abound."

Which does not make her anguish any more easier to bear, thought Captain Berhanu looking at the weeping woman. He sat down.

"Perhaps it is not the best time," he started out with a soft hesitant voice. "But I have to ask some background information for the investigation to proceed."

"Who could do such a terrible thing," the host's old wife said." He was such a quiet person. He kept to himself and his thoughts, the poor man."

The sister wailed loudly now calling the name of her

brother and asking God why He had to take her brother away from her. Captain Berhanu bent his head in deference and waited. When her cry and sobbing had subsided, he started out with his questions.

"What time did you come to the house?" he asked the sister.

"It was early morning, around seven thirty," she said between sobs. "I come over two times a week and check up on him. To cook for him, wash his cloths. He never asked for help and it broke my heart to see him a man cook for himself or wash his own clothes."

"He had no maid?"

"He refused to have one," said the sister. "He was one of those men who said one should help oneself."

"All by himself too," the older woman interjected. The maids will not stay unless they become 'chiin gered'." Maids of the loins, mistresses, the role that is played by maids traditionally, any children they bore shunned as "dikalas" or bastards. Captain Berhanu was reminded by his rural experience that there were also traditionally the "kosso missa", the name given to "slave" girls sent over with food to a man who had taken the bitter "iret" medicine on an empty stomach to extirpate the tapeworm from his insides (people paid the price in tapeworms for eating infected raw meat). The man was expected to sleep with her-- she was actually the lunch.

"Can you tell me his background? Family history?"

"We were five children in our family. Three died young and only the two of us remained. Our father was a civil servant. He died when we were quite young and it was our mother and our uncle who raised us. We all went to school. I cut short my education when I got married but Mulu went on to finish the University. He later worked at the Ministry of Agriculture. When this new government took over he was deprived of work and lived from his savings."

Captain Berhanu nodded. He knew the new rulers had arbitrarily deprived thousands of   their jobs and pensions. Ethnic politics and IMF orders.

"Was he jailed at any time?"

"People are jealous and vicious," said the sister. "More bones are broken by rumors than by sticks. He was denounced as a criminal and he was imprisoned for a while but there was no proof of any misdoing. He never hurt a fly."

Captain Berhanu was struck by the fact that this was exactly the phrase uttered by the butcher of a generation, former dictator Mengistu, who had fled to Zimbabwe. People who claim they never hurt a fly were not necessarily people who keep away from hurting or murdering human beings.

"Was he a member of any political organization?"

"Not that I know of," said the sister. "He loved his country and the poor, that's all."

Captain Berhanu, who did not believe her, did not pursue the subject. He asked instead: "Was he ever married?"

"No."

"Did he have children anyway?"

"Not that I know of. I wish he had one."

Captain Berhanu had enough of the sister. He knew she would not tell him any family secrets that, if any, he had to dig up all by himself. Most of the City folk measured their importance with the number of secrets in their possession-- everyone had or pretended to have secrets to guard, too many secrets. Mostly unimportant and insignificant in life, and rendered puny by the repressive State, most felt otherwise with the importance they enjoyed by themselves as guardians of what they call secrets.

"Who do you think would do such a terrible thing to your brother," he asked directly.

"God only knows," said the sister. "He bothered no one and had no property to draw anybody's eyes."

"These are bad times," said the old man. "People have lost their bearings, their sense of good and bad. Killing no longer requires a reason."

Captain Berhanu, who knew in the past of many people who killed for no reason at all other than sadistic cruelty, did not contradict the old man.

"Yet, nothing seems to have been robbed," he said instead. "And the mutilation…." At which the sister broke into a wild frenzy, striking at her chest, trying to pull out her hair. It took more than ten minutes for her to stop crying.

"I am sorry," said Captain Berhanu softly. "The more I know the faster I can apprehend the murderer."

"Bad times, bad times," said the old man. "Such cruelty. No wonder God has forgotten Ethiopia."

Captain Berhanu was of the opinion that if God did exist he had never heard of Ethiopia. "Such acts usually suggest jealous or aggrieved wives and lovers," he said to no one in particular.

"There was no woman to be jealous," said the sister. "Many a time I bothered him to get a wife, to give me a nephew or niece to spoil, but to no avail. He was ascetic, like a Bahtawi. He kept to himself and his books." And she broke into sobs again.

Minutes later Captain Berhanu left after murmuring the required words of condolences.

Captain Berhanu knew that the postmortem report would take days to arrive at his desk. When the Morgue at the Menilik Hospital, to where the corpse of Mulu would be taken, had first opened, there was no cold room and rats used to feast on rotting corpses. Later, a cold room has been installed but it was difficult to conduct an autopsy as relatives of the dead literally fought against any attempt to "open up and violate" their dead kin. During the military reign, when the Red Terror threw hundreds of corpses to the Morgue, autopsies were not even performed. The corpses were just too many and unceremoniously piled one on top of the other and given back to their kin only after they paid what was termed the bullet price: the cost of the number of bullets used by the soldiers and government murder squads to kill the victim. The pile of corpses was so high, a new job opportunity was opened for some people who would not mind the smell but would pull corpses out of the pile for relatives for a fee. Not many people shook the hands of anyone working at the morgue since they believed this would bring bad luck. Captain Berhanu drove back to his office and made some calls.

He made the first call to a longtime friend who had been close to the political actors of the violent times and now claimed he had "left it all" to be a businessman. Gugsa, as he was called, had an office near Arat Kilo and Captain Berhanu knew more than suspected that Gugsa's real business had little to do with consultancy of a commercial nature.

"I need some information on a person called Mulu Negew," said Captain Berhanu after the usual greetings. "He was a member of the group allied with the military regime and probably a Kebelle official too. You can check with former friends."

"Let us meet over lunch at Bafena," said Gugsa .

Captian Berhanu then called Public Prosecutor Getachew's office and asked for a copy of the file on Mulu Negew. Though he had identified himself, the Prosecutor's office refused to allow him to have access to the file. He walked to the office of his Colonel boss and had him call the Prosecutor's office. He got the permission as he had expected—to be listened to you did not need a reason but power and the right ethnic background. He left the building and drove over to the Public Prosecutor's office downtown. Half an hour later, he was sitting in the well-furnished office of the Chief Prosecutor's deputy.

A short and plump man with a goatee that made him look ridiculous, the deputy leafed through a thick file.

"Mulu Negew was a Kebelle official and a member of the main political group allied to the military regime. There are in these papers accusations and denunciations made alleging that he had killed or ordered the killing of a number of people. He was an educated man, therefore a cadre and not the run off the mill Kebelle official. But we were unable to get any concrete evidence or witness. "

Captian Berhanu was unable to trace a revealing accent in the man's speech. The deputy's face also did not exhibit any of the telltale tribal marks on the temples. His name, Tadele, was also ambiguous as it could belong to those who were not born in the North too. He decided to jump into the river.

"Was he released for political reasons?" he asked boldly.

The deputy looked straight at Captain Berhanu. The Captain noted that the man's eyes were empty of any feeling or message, like the eyes of dead sheep with which he had played when young.

"Political reasons, you say," the deputy asked. "What do you mean?"

Procrastinate, ask questions, and buy time to assess the question and its implications. Captain Berhanu, who knew the score like everyone else, understood.

"I got informed by some people that he was released because he had earlier joined the new political group called OPRO."

"I do not know about that," said the man cautiously. "But the file here shows that there could have been a case to take to court. But then again who am I to say? So many cases are pending and his may not have been that significant. The order for his release came from above and who am I to object?"

"Can you give me the file to read or tell me the main accusations?"

The deputy made no move to hand over the file. He said instead: "He was accused of torturing prisoners, murdering at least five others, causing the death of at least two prisoners in the Kerchiele.."

"Any names of the alleged dead?"

"Yes," replied the deputy. "Eshetu Tesema, Kinfu Isatu, Beshir Aden, Agere Kebede and Tafese Amsalu. The names of Fetlework Zena and Abeje Biru are also mentioned. In the latter's case, allegation is made that Mulu had him killed because he was the husband of Fetlework and Mulu wanted her all for himself."

"Did he get her?" asked the Captain taking note of the names.

"Did she have a choice," said deputy Tadele with a trace of some feeling. "He was a cadre, an official, she was the enemy of the State, a prisoner."

"Is there anything there that you think can help me with my case?"

The deputy just shrugged. "I don't know. My order is to brief you and not to hand you over the files. There is nothing that secret in the papers but we like to think there is. Mulu denied all the charges but I think you expect that from every sane Ethiopian accused of a crime. Maybe you should investigate the relatives of the alleged victims."

Captain Berhanu who had the same idea thanked the lawyer and left for his lunch rendezvous.

Bafena restaurant had definitely seen better days and the same could be said of Weizero Bafena, its owner. Bafena, person and location, were now tired and just a faded copy of their past. The woman was still fat but wrinkled and bent, the chairs and tables were still stable but hardly, there were curtains on the two windows but their colour had long gone away. Even the flies that buzzed around seemed tired. Yet, Bafena restaurant still served fine traditional food.

Captain Berhanu moved to the far end of the restaurant where he had spotted his friend Gugsa sitting with a bottle of Harar beer opened before him. The restaurant smelt of fried onions and meat.

"Never fat is your motto," said Gugsa extending his hand and getting up to greet his friend. Not all Ethiopians took being considered slim as a compliment.

"Begzier, begzier, sit down,' said the Captain shaking Gugsa's hand and pulling a chair to sit. He chose to order Bati beer, owned and made in Kombolcha by a French company. They ordered "Kitfo" and "Beyayinetu" for lunch.

After the waitress had served him beer and left, Captian Berhanu briefed his friend on the murder of Ato Mulu Negew. "Did you get anything?" he asked when he finished his account.

Gugsa, a slim and tall man in his fifties, smiled in a way that made his face look radiant and boyish. "Don't I always? Your Mulu Negew was quite somebody. A member of the group formed by the intellectuals who sold themselves to the military. A Kebele official, a political cadre. He was an active member of the Red Terror squads. He is accused of killing many people as many of them did at that time anyway. He was arrested by our new rulers along with Gesges Gebre Meskel, Asefa Girma and Tadele Mengesha who are accused of buying the skull of Ato Tefera Gebre Medhin for 15 Birr in an auction organized by the military government near Doro Gebeya, Amora Gedel region."

Captain Berhanu remembered the official policy of "Use Our Enemies Even When They Are Dead" and "Corpses to Serve the Revolution" which led to such strange practices as that of auctioning skulls, emptying the blood from a dying enemy to be stored in the Blood Bank to be of use for sick cadres or wounded officers, making parents pay the bullet price to collect the bullet riddled bodies of their children.

"Mulu was released since his new organization which is linked to the our ethnic- sensitive rulers appealed on his behalf. A friend of mine has more story to tell but I will tell you when we finish eating."

They rose to wash their hands and enjoyed, without any worry for cholesterol or the future of their hearts, Weizero Bafena's food which was soaked in butter. They ordered coffee in the end and Gugsa launched into the promised story.

"Mind you this is a story coming from someone who was in the movement and in prison, the Kerchiele, during the time Mulu Negew was linked to the military regime. Mulu grew up together with a boy called Abeje Biru. They were neighbors and went to the same elementary and secondary schools. In the university too, they were in the same faculty. When the Abyot, the February Revolution, broke out, Mulu was working in the Ministry of Agriculture while the Ethiopian Air Lines employed Abeje. The rather routine story of friendship gets spiced up like David and Saul's because there was a girl between the two. She was called Fetlework Zena and she was younger than both of them. She also lived in their neighborhood. By the time she was in high school, Abeje had started dating her and they were said to be in love. What both did not know was that Mulu was also desperately in love with her. When the 1974 Revolution struck to change the course of all our lives, she had already interrupted her university education, married Abeje and started working as secretary at the Commercial Bank.

You know friends do not always tread side by side and their hearts eventually do start to beat differently- close friends fall out. When the Revolution came, Mulu was drawn by the intellectual group allied to the military rulers while Abeje joined the Opposition that was incorrectly dubbed 'anarchist". At first, the two friends used to meet and argue the pros and cons of the military government and the stand one should take towards it. However, this did not last, could not last, as their differences were too serious. Mulu supported his group's position that one should take the huge task of changing this old country step by step, by nudging the military rulers to move foreword, by addressing constructive criticism to them while working with them in alliance. Abeje scoffed at this, as did his own group, arguing that the People did not choose the military to baby-sit the Revolution or any radical change. Hence, Abeje's belief in the call for a broad based transitional government to replace the military and to organize free elections. Of course, both Abeje and Mulu were leftists, if not Marxists, and both truly believed that one or the other of the Holy Books of this ideology vindicated their particular stand. The People, the Masses, the Oppressed, you could say not many really know who were these and what they thought of their self declared liberators or vanguards but you know where my sympathies stand. I say the difference was basically between those who really believed their own ideals and those who just pretended to do so. Let me come back to what interests you.

When the temporary peace ended and the bullets started flying, Abeje had to go underground. He was an active member and the government squads to which the likes of Mulu now belonged would have killed him instantly. I forgot to tell you that Abeje and Fetlework had a year old son by this time. The squads came to Abeje's house and not finding him took away his wife and son to the Kebelle prison. This was where Mulu reigned supreme, as he was the chairman, the squad leader and the political ideologue. He had around him demobilized soldiers and lumpen elements armed to the teeth and given killing powers. These were the frustrated detritus of the society and they took their revenge on all and sundry with viciousness. You know all that. To cut short a long story, Abeje was arrested some weeks later when a traitor denounced his hiding place to the police. Our country has a long history of patriots and traitors and those days could not be any different, could they? How can one shine and be valorized if the other is not around in all its perfidy? Abeje was brought before Mulu who not only supervised the torture of his old friend but also told him that his wife and son were already in custody. Yet, Abeje did not break. Every evening they took him out of the smelly and packed cell and tortured him. The whole works, akormaj to the sole of the feet, wefe- illala, the electrodes, you know it all. Mutilated and bloodied he refused to break; he did not expose his contacts and comrades. In the cell, he joined the other torture victims with their own rotting flesh, broken bodies but strong and unbreakable in spirit. They had faith and principles; they were not cynics and mercenary like most of us these days. Tortured and in pain, they sang the songs of their party, "Tiglunew Hiywete" specially, and angered their captors who tortured them even more.

Abeje knew that sooner or later Mulu and his goons would torture his wife and son in front of him so as to break him. This was what was worrying him most, not his pain, not his festering wounds. He had no cyanide pill hidden away somewhere in a body orifice or sewn into his clothes. Contact with the outside was also prohibited and difficult at that moment. The really intelligent man is the one who knows his limitations, his weaknesses, is he not? Abeje feared or knew he would break in the end if they brought over his wife and son to be tortured in front of him, as Mulu had planned actually though Abeje did not know for sure. At an evening's torture session, Abeje had the nerve to stumble and fall on the desk and to pick up a blade as he fell to the floor. He did not, like Zewdu Wolde Amanuel, use the blade to cut off the edges of his blanket to use it as a rope to hang himself with. Abeje had no blanket to cut. He just slit his wrists and died in the night. His comrades said there was a smile on his face and though they knew he was dying they did not try to dissuade him or to cry for help but sent him off into the night with a particularly emotional chorus of "Yetiglunew Hiywete".

If Mulu lost his victim in Abeje, he still had Fetlework and her son who were kept in another cell reserved for women. He made sure no one told Fetlework of her husband's death and he had her brought over to his office. Some say he just raped her outright, others allege that he made her agree by promising to release the husband that he knew she loved so deeply. It was not long before Fetlework knew that Abjee had died and that Mulu had used her. He continued to have sex with her for quite sometime and would have ordered her execution if only he had the time. But, powerful as he felt with the frenzy to decide on the life and death of so many prisoners, he was not the master of Time. Nor was he the chief or one of the leaders of his own organization. His bosses had fallen out with the military and had to run away to hide in their turn. He also ran and hid. Fetlework was taken to Kerchiele and she was again saved a possible execution because she was found to be pregnant."

They each ordered a glass of Cognac. Gugsa took more than a sip, grimaced and continued.

"It was not long before Mulu, finding the underground heat very, very hot, surrendered to the government, denounced himself and some of his friends, and through betrayal avoided long incarceration or punishment. As we say, a coward who tries to be the peacemaker in his own quarrel survives for his mother. The slimy part within him was not small, you could say. He did not know about Fetlework's condition. She was a broken woman, haggard and listless, just on the thin side of sane, but she had a lot of friends in the Kerchiele prison as female comrades of her husband were there on her side. They comforted her and helped her find the strength within her to resist. She had been thinking of suicide and of abortion but, a deeply religious woman, she resisted the devil and he was forced to leave her alone. Moreover, she had her son from Abeje whom she was still breast feeding. Her father had visited her in Kerchiele and begged her to give the boy to him but she had refused. The prison is no place to raise children in, had said her father. This country is no place to raise children in, she had replied to him. She became more politically conscious in prison but she kept her real pain to herself. Very few suspected that the baby in her womb was that of Mulu, many did not know at all and she did not talk about it to anyone but her father who came to visit her on all permitted days.

She gave birth to another boy in her cell and the women prisoners ululated and welcomed the baby though he had a criminal as a father. It is here we come to the end of the story as my informant was released but he told me that her son had died in prison."

"And Fetlework? I heard she was finally executed?"

"Bad luck," said Gugsa. "And it was plenty in those days. A condemned woman prisoner whose parents had paid the necessary bribe to save her from death was saved while the prison wardens killed Fetlework instead and gave her the other woman's name. The child was handed over to Fetlework's father who was warned not to hold a wake for his daughter, or else."

"So, Mulu did not have her killed?"

Gugsa shrugged. "Having someone killed requires you do what? He got her to Kerchiele, didn't he? He did not have to take her before the firing squad. He placed her in front of a speeding car, didn't he?"

Captain Berhanu nodded in understanding.

"You have her father's address?"

Gugsa told him and said: "I know you have your job but Mulu got what he deserved. Justice delayed is better than justice denied. Whosoever punished him needs to be rewarded."

Captain Berhanu kept his opinion on the matter to himself. As usual when they met for lunch or drinks, Gugsa the self-declared business- man covered the bill.

Come, let us talk this over, says the Lord, no matter how deep the stain of your sins, I can take it out and make you as clean as the conscience of a new born baby. As Captain Berhanu drove to the house of the father of Fetlework, he pondered over crime, sin and punishment. He was, like most of his country-folk, very much of a believer in the whole concept of vendetta. A wrong must be avenged, redressed. A murderer must be punished. But who is the murderer and who the victim? Or, should the whole thing be left to God for him to sort out, as he was responsible for the whole mess in the first place? Captain Berhanu did not really believe in God but he was very much used to the idea of a God and the convenience of having someone on whom all can be pinned. When he had been assigned to a rural police station, he had come face to face with crude and base cruelty, seen murders for little or no reason at all and vendettas that lasted more than two decades and in the end the victim had nothing to do with the original crime or perpetrators. Is the killer of Mulu a murderer or an avenger? Is there a difference between the two at all? Captain Berhanu had no answer to these questions that had plagued him over the years. Was it ever right to wash off the stain of a sin? Was it ever right for man to be in a position to play God? He knew the Bible almost by heart since his late mother used to drag him to every church and monastery she trekked to. Vengeance is mine, said the Lord, but can the aggrieved human being not lend a hand at all? Would God even mind or care? He had no easy answers but he knew that he did not like the Truth and Reconciliation thing they were having down in South Africa. Who needs to know the bitter truth? Reconcile with murderers? NO.

The house of the father of Fetlework was located in the eastern part where the most rundown and slum areas of the dilapidated city were found. The old man himself opened the door and invited the Captain in after he had introduced himself. His hair full and totally white, the old man was dressed in clean but shabby khaki shirts and trousers and hardly showed surprise when Captain Berhanu introduced himself as a policeman.

The old man lived in a one room kiosk-like house. Two chairs (one wobbly as Captain Berhanu found out as he sat), a small table, a sagging bed at one corner, a photo of a pretty girl on the wall alongside the picture of a white Mother Mary holding baby Jesus, also white.

"What can I do for you?" The old man had a strong voice. Captain Berhanu looked him straight in the eyes. Small, brown eyes, soft and suggesting vulnerability. Captain Berhanu, who knew his Ethiopians to an E, concluded this old man must be a tough and hard person.

He told the old man about the death of Mulu Negew (no flicker of recognition in the old man's eyes) and took the story softly along to suggest the need for him, from the CID-Homicide, to talk (just routine, you know) to your grandson, the son of Weizero Fetlework (was she the pretty woman I see in that photo? Yes? I guessed as much. How sad.")

The old man sat still. The silence between them weighed heavily but neither was uncomfortable having been used all their lives, like most of their country folk, to such moments. In the end, the old man broke the silence.

"I really do not see what my grandson has to do with the dead man. He was just a baby when all the things you talked about happened. He cannot remember the pain. He does not remember his mother for that matter. "

"Does he live here with you?"

"No," replied the old man sweeping a brief look at the small room. "He works in the Ministry of Education for a pittance they call a wage. He visits me from time to time."

"How can I find him?"

"He lives in the Arat Kilo area," said the old man and gave Captain Berhanu the exact Kebele and house number.

"Did you know Ato Mulu by the way?"

"Of course I did. We lived in the same Kebele at the time. I knew his mother too. A quiet boy he was. Who would have imagined he would turn into such a terrible man afterwards. The ways of the Lord are so mysterious. Like that fellow Girma Kebede who bayoneted the eight month pregnant Daro Negash-- an ordinary young boy suddenly turning into a monster—how can you explain it?"

"Most of the murderers I have met are fellows you can describe as ordinary," said Captain Berhanu. "We have perhaps in all of us this capacity to be someone else altogether. On my part, I think the line between ordinary and strange, killer and victim, sane and insane has been blurred for long now."

"May God have mercy on us all then. If the wolf does not have to put on the skin of a lamb to look different, then we are in deep trouble."

Weren't we always, Captain Berhanu said to himself.

"Who do you think would kill Ato Mulu? In this way, I mean?" Captain Berhanu was fishing aimlessly.

The old man did not respond immediately and when he did it was in the usual roundabout way which reminded Captain Berhanu of the saying: ask the mule who his father is and he will say my uncle is a horse. It took Captain Berhanu more than a day to really understand what the old man was actually trying to say.

"What we sometimes suffer is nothing compared to the suffering we may have given to others," said the old man softly. "It becomes all the worse when we do the harm deliberately and not inadvertently for we cannot even say sorry and get our apology accepted in good faith. The cross one is condemned to carry is often unbearable. The life of one's child is the most precious as God proved by giving us his Son's life to wash off our sins. Who amongst us is Christian enough to say the same? Happy is the man who doesn't give in and do wrong when tempted, wrote St. James in the Bible. Can I resist temptation? Can you? Temptations big and small devour us. Ato Mulu sinned. Who killed Ato Mulu and sinned in turn?

Maybe he killed himself. I do not mean he took his own life. I mean to say his evil deeds may have provoked, led to his death in the end. As you said, thieves do not cut off the organ of the person they rob though these days I hear wild things are happening in this cursed city. Someone with a grievance? Maybe. With a big wound I will even say. But it may not have to be from the distant past, no. "

"Those were Armageddon-days," said Captain Berhanu. "Bloody times".

The old man nodded in agreement. He said: "Old fathers like me denounced their own children, and sent them to the butchers. Thugs were let loose on innocent people. We were humiliated so much as to sing the praise of the military scums slaughtering our own babies. We were forced to confront our cowardice and to cuddle it. So, after you have succumbed to your own fear, what face is left for you, what honor or self-respect? Nothing. Who can blame anyone else for something that happened at that time? Not me anyway. If at all Ato Mulu's death was a result of a vendetta, it may very well be for something he did in the recent past."

Captian Berhanu thanked the old man for his time and views and left the tiny house and the foul smelling Kebelle not anymore enlightened than he had been before.

He did not find the son of Fetlework at the Ministry of Education. They told him he had left off for the afternoon claiming he was feeling sick. A drive to the son's house did not bear fruit: it was a two- roomed house in a compound of four such houses sharing a common out house. A woman sitting outside of one of the houses cooking over a coal stove informed him that Ato Dagim Abeje, the son, was not at home. Dagim lived alone.

Next morning, Captain Berhanu came to the office rather late but the report from the post mortem examination was not yet in. Lieutenant Solomon had also come and gone to pursue one of the wild cases the men on top threw down at him. Captain Berhanu came late because he had earlier driven to the house of Dagim and caught the young man as he was preparing to leave for work. Their conversation had been brief. Dagim claimed he never knew or met Ato Mulu and had avoided digging deep into the story of his mother and father and how they had died. Let bygones be bygones, they lived their lives as they saw fit and I will live my own, was what the son said. A difficult but wise decision. The less one dwells on catastrophe, the less one may suffer. Captain Berhanu could understand the sentiment but he was perturbed by Dagim's total lack of interest in Mulu or how and why he died. A tall young man in his early twenties, with eyes full of life, how could he lose all interest in his own past?

"Where were you yesterday early morning?" The young man had smiled at the Captain's question. "Am I a suspect?" Routine question. "I was here in the morning and my neighbors may have seen me leave for work at the usual time". The Captain had later checked with the neighbors and they had confirmed they had seen Dagim wash up, use the out- house and later leave. In early morning, yes, his usual time, before eight.

Captain Berhanu was checking his "Current" file when there was a knock at the door and Sergeant Lemma came in and saluted formally.

"The full post mortem report is not ready, sir," he told Captain Berhanu. "But the chief doctor said that he could tell us that the victim died of knife wound with one stab to the heart being the fatal one and that he had died in the night before and not in the morning."

"What?" Captain Berhanu did not hide his surprise.

"Yes sir. The doctor said the victim was killed probably sometime between ten pm and midnight the previous evening."

Of course! Captain Berhanu silently cursed and blamed himself for assuming the man had died in the morning just because he was found then by his sister and the corpse did not smell. He also cursed at the technical team. If the Abadinas of old, the professionals, had been on the scene they would have judged from the rigor mortis the time of death. Damn! He drove to the Ministry of Education, found Dagim in his office and posed his question.

"Where were you yesterday evening between ten pm and midnight?"

"So, he did not die in the morning as you had said," said Dagim with a mocking smile.

Too many youngsters watch too much TV, Captain Berhanu noted to himself.

"I was at home and dead asleep by midnight,' said the young man.

"Anyone to vouch for that?"

"My neighbors may testify I was in by eight."

"Can they testify you never left?"

"I wouldn't know. You have to ask them but I tell you I was asleep by midnight."

Returning to the house of Dagim, Captain Berhanu found two women of the compound. Both said they had seen Dagim come in at eight, his light was on till at least ten thirty (said one) or eleven (said another). Thank you, said a frustrated Captain Berhanu. Thank you, Captain, they both said. Can you give me a lift to the bus station, asked one of the women? He agreed and she put on her "netela" and came out with him to his battered Volkswagen. Polite behavior made inconsequential talk necessary within the confines of the small Volkswagen. He even laughed at one of her witty remarks on how the modern girls are "open" in more ways than one. And this led to her subsequent comment that his employers must exploit him since they do not seem to pay him well enough to afford a bigger or newer car. Mind you, I know you are better off than Dagim, for example, the woman then went on to say. He does not own a car though he had borrowed one the other night. If he had been paid enough he could have rented a bigger house and brought in his grandfather to live with him, no? The woman gossiped on till he dropped her at the place she wanted. She would have been surprised to know that Captain Berhanu had listened to her closely and was, as he drove back to his office, singing her praises. He felt he was at last seeing some light. Motive was there, and now possibly opportunity too.

He decided to drive back to his office and to send a detective with a car to bring over Dagim. An hour later, Dagim was ushered into his office.

"Sit down, sit down." Captain Berhanu's smile was not reciprocated.

"Being visited or summoned by the police will not endear me to my superiors," the young man complained as he sat.

"I apologize," said the Captain. "Police and mother in-laws-- you can avoid one if you do not get married but the police are always with you."

"With?"

Captain Berhanu laughed aloud.

He said: "I summoned you to ask you further questions. Did you borrow a car on the evening in question?"

"I had. I was out drinking with a friend who had more than the usual and wanted to pass the night with a bar- girl. I took his car to drive back home and picked him up the next morning and gave him back his car." Dagim told the Captain the name of the friend and his place of work. Check with him please.

"I am not doubting the veracity of what you say. What worries me is the possibility that you may have sneaked out of your house around ten thirty or so, drove over to Ato Mulu's house to murder him."

Visibly unperturbed, the young man laughed. "And why should I have done that?"

"To avenge your father and mother," said Captain Berhanu. "Vendetta. The common Ethiopian response in such a situation."

"That may have been so in your time," said Dagim making the Captain feel old. "Principles to die for, courage, sacrifice, vendettas, underground, cyanide pills...and such are things of your generation, Captain. Not mine. We are the post- Red Terror generation. We survive, quietly and without great expectations. We are neither martyrs nor rebels. The ideals and dreams have perished with our dead parents. If the price is right we can sell off our mothers. Ask any young man queuing outside the American embassy for a visa and he will tell you.

Ato Mulu did not do anything to me. Even if he had, I would not have the will or the courage to do to him what you said had been done to him. You must understand we are cowards, we have been turned into cowards, I am a coward and not ashamed of it at all."

"I pity you all if what you say is true. If you have no dreams and ideals it means you are all shriveled and old long before you pass twenty-one. Youngsters like you died for this country?"

"Precisely," said the young man with a smile. "They died. And who is around? People who would not give you a cent let alone their lives. Who survived? The flexible many; the opportunist ones with no rigid principles, with no firmly held conviction or pride to make them sacrifice their precious lives. The killers are alive and well. The victims died-- but for whom?"

Captain Berhanu chose to ignore the last question. He said instead: "the likes of Takele Welde Hawaryat and other patriots left you this country."

"Who?"

"Yes, who?" said Captain Berhanu sadly. "To come to the point though, let me tell you that long experience has taught me that most killers are actually cowards."

The young man smiled. "I did not even know where he lived. To tell you the truth, if Ato Mulu did kill my parents it was because it had to be."

"Are you turning fatalist on me?"

"I believe. I am a Christian. It is not fatalism. One shouldn't clog one's memory with hatreds that have gone sour and cold over the years. They were in opposite camps and my father would have probably killed him if he had had the chance. It is all in the past and distant for me. I was just a baby at the time too."

"But a baby in prison," said the Captain. "An orphan."

"I did not kill the man. Can I go now, please"?

"You can go," said Captain Berhanu, adding bluntly, "go, but we both know that you did kill that man."

"You accuse without proof? Isn't that unprofessional?"

The Captain had to agree that it was. After Dagim left, the Captain lit a cigarette forgetting his decision to stop smoking. He blew smoke in the air and thought about the case. He was now close to certain that the young man had committed the vendetta. The cutting off the penis must have been to get even with what had been done to his mother, to chop off the instrument and symbol of her humiliation and shame. Captain Berhanu recalled the words of the grandfather of Dagim. Maybe Mulu caused his own death? Heaven knows we are not a people who forget or forgive easily, mused the Captain. We can carry a grudge for decades, nurture and protect it from any lapse of memory, water it with hate till it consumes our very soul and we finally succumb to the temptation. Vendetta. When wronged, we strike back. We do not resist the devil but become one with him, turn into his instruments. It was at this point in his thoughts that the question suddenly popped up in his head. Who told the boy? How did Dagim know? The Captain knew that the few friends of Gugsa and old comrades of Dagim's father, who had the slim chance to survive, would not inform the young boy of what had been done to his mother. Not in such details anyway. Who then?

The old man let him into the small room that smelt of coffee and incense.

"I imagined you would be back," said Fetlework's father after they had sat.

"Why?"

"Aren't you a policeman? Excuse me for my words but you all are like dogs with its tail in its mouth. You turn and turn around. Unable to fathom the truth you return to the simple, the comfortable. You are also like priests, more at ease with the facile, the dogma, the explainable."

"You have had much direct experience with the police?"

"Am I not an Ethiopian? How can I avoid Kebele and the police? You are like the 'chika shums' in our villages. Let us leave that and do tell me what you want from me this time."

"I want to ask why?"

"Why what?"

"I think you know," said Captain Berhanu. "You must be the one who told him all and prepared him for the act."

"The act? Why do you say the act? If you mean the murder, say so. Say the murder. No need to cover it up. Murder should be named and its ugliness emphasized if you want people to learn to avoid it."

"The murder then," agreed the Captain.

"I did not send my grandson to do any murder," said the old man firmly. "I am on the verge of meeting my Creator and I have enough sins to atone for without adding such a heavy one on my already-bent shoulders."

"I do not think you would consider a vendetta a burden. On the contrary, a final relief, a good farewell present."

The old man let a flicker of a smile appear on his face.

"You see," the captain started to explain," there is no other explanation. Not that I can think of anyway. The boy has the motive and the opportunity. The cutting of the penis can also be plausibly explained only in this way, as the dead man had no women friends to fill in as jealous suspects. Who prepared the boy? Who else but a retributive grandfather who cannot forget what had happened to his one and only daughter."

The old man looked down at his own old shoes and remained quiet. Captain Berhanu went on: "let me take your time and tell you a story. It was while I was posted in a rural no man's land that I came across it. A family of four was found murdered, shot to death by what I found out later was a bolt rifle they called Mauser, a husband, wife and two sons not more than ten years old. Nothing was robbed; they were poor anyway. It did not take me long to find out who the murderer was. It was a man who had bitterly quarreled with the dead man some months back. The reason was not even significant but the would be victim had descended upon the would-be killer's farm and uprooted the lemon tree he had nurtured over the years. This was enough to drive the man crazy. He retaliated by shooting the whole family to death. For one lemon tree four human lives. And the killer had no regrets at all."

The old man smiled. "To grow a lemon tree takes a lot of effort, patience and time."

"Like a daughter".

"If you will. A daughter means love too. But what drives people to uncontrollable rage is not easily discernible."

"Yet, revenge, which we all consider inevitable, could be avoided," said Captain Berhanu unconvincingly. "It is not usually a spur of the moment thing. If it is true it involves passion it is but a cold one. The time we take to plan for the revenge can also be used to think of another way, perhaps."

"Well there comes a time when the victim says enough is enough and anger takes over," said the old man. "As we say, even the broken serf or the slave will reach the time to say enough! I have been aggrieved. Moreover, the spirits have to be calmed. I am not sure if the moral of your story concerns that we kill for little or nothing at all or if you are trying to tell me that we are all after revenge."

"What do you think?"

"To kill without reason is, for me, profane."

It was the turn of Captain Berhanu to smile. "Where have you been living? This is a country where most murders have little or no motive." The Captain, who believed that most people would tell the truth or own up to a mistake if only they could find a mask to cover the shame and responsibility, continued with the conversation.

"Some people will not kill anyone they did not know enough to hate, others commit murder on strangers. You surely remember the story of the son of the rich Ras who killed a number of peasants when he used them for target practice. He had a reason as far as he was concerned since the rulers and the wealthy never consider our lives worth anything. Can we compare the life of a human being to a lemon tree?"

"The importance and worth depends on the aggrieved," said the old man. "He who wounds may forget but the wounded never does, as we say. To the killer you mentioned, the lemon tree was more important. His loss was unbearable for sure. Who are we to judge or complain since we all exalt the shifta, the outlaw? When a blood debt is collected, we celebrate. That has been our way for centuries."

"The glamorization of murder," commented the Captain. "A society that justifies murder in one way or another promotes lawlessness."

"If there ever was the Law," countered the old man. "Do you think the rule of law exists in our city? You are a policeman and you have your work but I do not think it has anything to do with law or justice. In our country, the Law has never been respected by those entrusted with applying it. Every fool knows this."

Captain Berhanu chose to ignore the jibe.

He said instead: "Ato Mulu was detained and released?"

"Precisely," agreed the old man. "Justice was denied. The law itself was ignored. My daughter and her husband did not count."

"But can killing Ato Mulu bring solace to them?"

"Who says vendetta is for the victims' good? I do not believe their souls are roving restless till the blood debt gets settled. Vendetta is for the living. It is to deal with our loss and pain."

"But vengeance is mine has said the Lord."

"Maybe we are philistines," said the old man shaking his head. "God Himself took revenge when he deemed it necessary, didn't he? We worship a jealous and vengeful God. Who would have believed in God if he were not so? No one. It is the God of punishment, of floods, the God who destroyed Sodom and Gomorrah, who smashed icons and chased profaners out of his temple. That is our God. We need fear to believe in anything"

Captain Berhanu decided to avoid arguing theology with the old man. "He still took revenge directly," he said instead. "Not through another person."

The old man stared into he eyes of the Captain as if he was trying to read into the policeman's very soul.

"You think you have fathomed it all?" he asked finally.

"No, I am asking you to enlighten me," replied the Captain.

"I think Dagim killed Ato Mulu and I believe you put him up to it. Your own grandson."

"You will not get confirmation of what you say from me but let me remind you we are soaked in crime and murder as a people. Our rulers get to the palace only after killing innocents beyond count. Those in power and with riches kill in one way or another. You even kill people you never met which I think is worse than murdering someone you knew and could at least hate. Who killed your Ato Mulu? Who knows? Justice is usually done by hands that have been chosen by God."

"You know I may have to arrest you both?"

"If that is what you have to do, then do it,' said the old man calmly." We all must do our duty."

"I ask again why the boy? Why didn't you do it yourself? Isn't passing one's duty to someone else a travesty of the rules?"

"Whose rules? Sons avenge their parents as far as I know. Sons can also kill their parents as you very well know."

It was the turn of Captain Berhanu to stare at the old man who stared back at him, eyes unflinching. Cold and dead eyes.

"No!" shouted Captain Berhanu. "You couldn't!"

The old man, who understood, just smiled, a smile of victory and contentment.

"No!" repeated Captain Berhanu as what had dawned on him sunk deeper. "You didn't, did you?"

The old man said nothing. The smile on his face mocked at the Captain.

"You did, didn't you?" said the Captain. "You sent the son to kill his own father."

"The Lord said I will not stand silent, I will repay, repay them not only for their sins but also for that of their fathers. Isaiah chapter 65,verse 6. »

"I do not think you are fit to quote the Bible,' said Captain Berhanu angrily. "You have no faith at all."

The old man smiled again. "Why do you say that? Aren't we Ethiopians passionate even in our heresies and over our failures, let alone our victories?"

"What victory? Sending a son to kill his own father? You are a cruel old man, a sinner."

"Yes," said the old man. "Sometimes the way of sin is the only way."

"For what?"

"For one's salvation, maybe not in heaven but here on earth. I will sleep calmly from now on."

"What about the boy? He is still your grandson. For God's sake, he is the son of your daughter."

"Who was raped and driven to her death by the dog," said the old man calmly. "Too bad the son had to be born and even worse her first son had to die. I raised this one telling him his father was Abeje and that Mulu has murdered his parents. Not many people knew the one who died in prison was her first son. The cell-mates who knew or suspected died like her. I had no difficulty convincing this one his father was Abeje. So, the boy did not kill his father, not in his mind anyway. He believes he killed the man who murdered his parents and the man did cause his mother's death."

"You think you are clever, don't you?" The anger and contempt of the Captain was loud in his voice.

"I had thought you intelligent," said the old man, "but you disappoint me. This has nothing to do with being clever or cruel, nothing at all. I hated the man who defiled my daughter and led her to her death. Nothing done to him was enough to calm the shrieking rage and the burning hate in me. Having him killed by his own son seemed proper to me. Mind you, he didn't even know he was being killed by his own son, I saved him from that."

"How generous! Did he know he was being killed by Fetlework's son?"

"The boy told him before killing him. That he had to know. Otherwise, the vendetta would have been incomplete, flawed. Now, do your duty and arrest me. I am ready to take the whole blame and anything you say to the contrary will not be believed by anyone. If you really feel pity for the boy, do as I say. Leave him out of this. I never intended for him to know he killed his own father; there is no reason which dictates you should tell him. What I did you would have done in my place. It is our way."

Captain Berhanu looked at the calm old man who sat unperturbed. He realized that even after so many years of police work the ways and actions of his country folk never ceased to amaze him. He feared the old man had said the truth: maybe most Ethiopians would have done like him. The "Bekel", the vengeance was all, the more cruel the vendetta, the more the satisfaction. Captain Berhanu was not sure of what he had to do now. Once again justice had shrouded herself in ambiguous garbs and challenged him to understand. The old man has usurped his own God and taken vengeance. Captain Berhanu had no God to betray and his certitude on right and wrong had abandoned him long ago. What was now his duty?

"Can I have some water?" he finally asked the old man.

The "Anderibi" Story

On the day I was born, my father tried to kill me twice while my mother broke down and just wept. It was the mid- wife who saved my life. She was also the only one to ululate to herald my birth. And me? I cried, as all newborn babies do, but had I known what awaited me I would have shed even more bitter tears. The irony is that it wouldn't have made any difference at all—it is that kind of country.

"It is God's will," said the mid-wife restraining my father.

"It is the devil's work," my father disagreed forgetting that I was his son. "What will the Emperor say?"

The Emperor, of course, not only did not know my poor father existed but actually cared more for his Chihuahua and other pets than he did for the millions he called his "loyal subjects".

"God will understand," said the midwife diplomatically and confidently, as if she, like dictator Idi Amin, had a direct and private line with the Almighty. Having often delivered babies with all types of deformities, she surely knew how to handle devastated parents. "He sent him to you for a purpose".

"Yes, to shame me." My father was desperate. "To punish me for my sins."

"Eyob was tested," the midwife reminded him.

My father was a man with little of the patience that had characterized Eyob or Job and he tried to strangle me again. With such a welcome, no wonder my life turned out to be a total mess and an example of God's unexplained penchant for cruelty. My father, whose first child I was, abandoned my mother and me two months after my birth as if my condition reflected on him and made him lose face in the society.

Had I the possibility or the intelligence, I would have been born in another country where oddities like me are tolerated and, as someone told me of India, revered.

I was born a hermaphrodite, neither a man nor a woman, an uncertainty in a country where the ability to entertain ambiguity has always been considered dangerous despite the age- old tradition of intrigue and aversion to blunt or direct talk. I was thus a cursed child, an unbearable shame to my parents, a horrid being to be categorized not along but worse than those born without limbs or joined to one another. My mother did not let me forget I was peculiar, not normal, a "wendagered" as she called me, a male-female, a He-woman, a She-man. She warned me never to piss, relieve myself or be nude in the presence of other children. I had a small penis-like organ and a vagina. Afraid of the world before I even got to know it, confronted by an identity crisis even before I had grown up to be confused by life, I faced the future with my heart in my mouth.

I never undressed in public nor did I piss in the presence of other children but they knew. They always know, don't they? Children are pests. Whoever said children are like angels has never met those creatures with wings. I can tell you how vicious and cruel children can be. They are mostly ignorant; say unconscious, and what is taken as innocence is actually their inborn viciousness. Children enjoy the pain of others. Have a hunchback, be a cripple, have any visible physical defect and, little and illiterate as they may be, they will come up with a song that will crush you. "Wendagered who are you really/ do you stand or sit to pee, who are you/can we see?"-- and this was the least offensive one. When I went to the priest's school to learn to read and finish the Pslams (and to endure the sadistic beatings of the priest-teacher in whose honor we all sang "beneta gurero tej yinkorkor, begna gurero atint yikerker"- may mead and honey pour down our teacher's throat/while a big bone gets stuck in ours-), it did not take the children long to know I had something "wrong", that I was not like them. Maybe it was the way I carried myself though I wore shorts like boys, maybe my refusal to pee with them in public or to shove my penis in a hole in the ground in which they poured water to make it moist and they put their little penises in and out in an imitation of what grown up men are supposed to do with women. Anyway, they did not take time to know. I was referred to as a "wendeagered" by almost all by the time I entered the primary school. My mother had called me Gero, which was neither a boy's name nor that of a girl's, and thereby safe by being something you cannot pin down to one category or meaning. You would think this would have satisfied them all since a society that has made secrets and imprecision a national pastime would be expected to understand, but no. Was I a boy or a girl? Mind you, this is a society that considers homosexuality a sickness and where even many of the self- declared revolutionaries openly declare, if they ever come to power, the firing squad will deal with such elements. No matter if the macho society did have quite a few such "sick people" and not all of them were dwelling in monasteries and Koranic schools.

My life in school was hell on earth. As I said, children are not innocent or pure—only ignorant and without social restraints. Hence, their cruelty was intense and relentless. Beaten and punished cruelly, as a matter of routine, by their parents, teachers and elders, denied even the smallest of rights, bugged by lice and fleas, poor and miserable and frightened by the society at large, their viciousness increased many folds.

The epithets they hurled at me pricked more than porcupine needles are supposed to hurt and worse than the vaccination scratches we were being given at school. Bear it as I did, the dam often burst open at night when, in the dark, on my own flea- ridden mattress on the floor, the insults came back to me and pierced my reserve and I had to sob till sleep finally overtook me. Children can exhibit more wanton cruelty than a frenzied mob with machetes.

My mother took me out of school when I begun my sixth grade.

"You know the midwife who saved you from your father's wrath did say God must have a purpose for you", she had said. "I do not want you to waste away or kill yourself because others make you suffer." My mother, who never remarried and who took care of me by selling onions, tomatoes, injera and spices at the local market called "Gulit" never ceased to love me. A mother's love is bottomless, it is said, and my mother never gave me any reason to doubt it. I believe the unsung heroes of our country are actually our mothers, not the so-called heroes who were in most cases armed and uncouth men having a good time and free food at the expense of others. When the so-called Revolution came in 1974 to compound my problems and to cause the massacre of so many youths, it was the mothers who bore the burden. Many were jailed as the stupid regime held them responsible for the acts of their children, many more were tortured so that their revolutionary children would break or confess, not quite a few opened their doors in the morning to go to Church and found the dead bodies of their sons or daughters thrown nearby. They were forbidden to weep, to shed tears and many wept inside their empty wombs. Thousands of mothers suffered and bore the pain; they seemed to have an endless reserve of patience and resilience. Their off- springs disappeared without a trace and not knowing whether they were dead or alive they worried themselves to death and tried to find solace in prayers and devotions. I would not have survived if my mother were not around to protect and comfort me.

Yet, I also had to learn to take care of myself. Self-pity was not for me. I saw nothing wrong in me, I had never asked to be born this way-- no great deal if I had an extra sex organ when others had only one. I was determined to survive and this meant then I should not stay indoors as my mother advised. I deliberately chose to go out, to walk around, to roam. Zuret, it was called, an entirely purposeless walking around. I heard later some countries consider it a punishable offense but in our city, where more people were unemployed and on the streets rather than at work, zuret was a therapeutic and unavoidable activity. I hear some Ethiopian exiles still do it even in downtown Washington, the capital city of America itself. My decision to survive demanded that I find a way to tame the boys in my street. There was specially one bully called Mesfin who was particularly vile and pushed the others to insult and taunt me.

My chance came one day when I was going to the nearest souk (shop) to buy some sugar for my mother. From a distance I saw Mesfin and his band of boys standing in a circle and looking down at something. As I approached, I saw that there was a mouse-trap on the ground with an obviously very trapped and very frightened mouse in it. Mesfin looked up and spotted me.

"Hey, you who wear trousers, come and touch this rat if you are a real male?" he shouted contemptuously. All the others looked at me with smiles of derision and contempt on their faces. I knew they were all scared of touching the rat. I was also frightened but I knew if I ran I would be losing the chance of a lifetime.

"Who has a match?" I asked boldly.

Mesfin pulled a pack from his pocket and handed it to me. The boys opened up the circle to let me approach the mouse-trap. I calmly picked a torn piece of cloth from the ground and taking the tail of the mouse wrapped the cloth around it. I knew what I was going to do was cruel and despicable but I had to survive, to win, and I really did not care if this has to be at the price of the mouse's life. I lit the torn cloth and opened the trap to let the mouse ran in fright followed by its own burning tail. The boys roared in laughter with Mesfin joining in reluctantly. Not only had I dared to touch the mouse, I had also excelled them in malevolence and sadism. Young as I was, I had instinctively realized that one gets on top in the society not by being gentle and considerate but by trampling on others and by just being evil. Sadism paid, it still does.

I had tamed the boys with whom I now started to roam the streets. I became just plain Gero and no more "wendagered". I was turning thirteen when my mother died on me. She failed to wake up in the morning and she was just dead. The street whispered that I had broken her heart and killed her. A "godolo", a freak, I have often heard them call me. They sympathized with the father who had abandoned me. The blame was all on me, the society hated underdogs, the patriots who fought against the Italian invaders were slaughtered by the villagers, their own compatriots, whenever they had to retreat. A conformist and uncomfortable society.

An aunt took me in after the funeral of my mother. The aunt sold tella and tej beverages to men. I found out soon enough she was also a prostitute on the side. She also got some money as an alkash, a professional tear- jerker. She was hired to make people cry for the dead at funerals and while she whipped up the funeral crowd, especially the women, to a frenzy of chest beating and hair pulling, she hardly ever shed a tear herself. After all, she did not know most of the dead she had to wail for to get paid. It said much on the society and the times that close relatives had to be goaded and provoked to weep for a dead kin. Most of the time I was on the street anyway and since she lived not far from where I had lived with my mother I continued with the Mesfin gang of boys. I came home only to grab some food if I could get it and left immediately afterwards.

Two days before I turned fourteen, my aunt sold me to a man for fifty Birr which was at that time a lot of money, say five hundred now. You could buy a sheep at five Birr and not pay more than a hundred times like we do now. As people are wont to say, bad todays make terrible yesterdays look gentler and much as I hated those days I look back fondly at them. To come back to my story, the man had claimed, as I was to learn later on, that a wizard had told him to have sex with a "wendagered" if he was to be cured from his ailment that I never came to know. The fateful night when I returned home from the street, the man was with my aunt. He was middle aged, with a big belly and a breath that smelt so bad that I felt even the fleas and bed bugs had fled from our humble abode.

"Go into the bed room", my aunt ordered me though she had always warned me not set foot in her bedroom lest I jinxed it.

As I went in, the man rushed in after me and holding me by my tiny waist threw me on the bed. My attempt to scream was stifled by his rough and broad hand that clamped on my mouth. He slapped me twice and as he breathed on me I almost fainted. Warned of more beating if I opened my mouth, I kept still as he took of my clothes. The sight of my small penis did not shock him. "Oh, God, the miracle-maker," he said in awe as he took off his trousers and pulled out his own huge organ. It was over in a few minutes, sharp pain, defilement and humiliation. I was soiled and robbed of what I assumed to be my innocence. My future was also set.

Yes, I became a prostitute in a puritan society that strangely tolerated the practice, with my aunt taking the role of my pimp. Word spread that I was a "medhanit" (a "medicine"), a "cure" for many ailments. My aunt bribed the witch doctor nearby to send more clients. I was kept busy. She bought me new clothes and the perfumes made by Hunbelew Mera, you know the stingy millionaire who used to wear shabby clothes and torn shoes and whose entire fortune was confiscated by the military government. I learnt to enjoy it all specially the power I had over the men who approached me with awe and paid much money for just few minutes of pleasure with me. On the street, none of them gave any sign of knowing me at all, passing by with hurried walks, eyes cast in any direction but towards me. I learnt that most men were hypocrites, ready to sin so long as no one knew or seemed to know about it. In public, all of them would surely join a mob stoning a "bushti"/homosexual/ or so- called "godolo"s / freaks like me to death. If you ignore your conscience no sin is heavy. Isn't it true also that a sin repeated is soon considered as a good act, as our saying puts it?

And then the Revolution came. It came for some and it came against some. Those who had thought the Revolution was theirs were soon to find out that the Revolution had a special appetite for its own children. Youngsters with ideals gave their lives for those they called the people—I was not sure if they considered me amongst this amorphous mass- but they were really good hearted and quite naïve. They did not know their country or their people. Where ruthlessness defined the ordinary man they sought to find magnanimity. The soul of our people, I had long concluded, was a labyrinth, dark and fetid, filled with the dregs of hidden sins and unfulfilled but devious intentions. The young chased their own moon and stars and dared to dream when they should have been glad to be allowed to cling to their nightmare. The military took over and some of my rich and hidden customers went to jail, not because they had relations with me, oh no, but for the simple reason that they were part of the overthrown ruling class. Do you see how high I was flying before the cursed Revolution came to deprive me of my "cash boats" as my Kat-chewing friends would have called them?

I wonder if all Revolutions crown hypocrisy. Ours claimed to be puritan through and through. Imagine soldiers who rape and rob at will suddenly claiming to be guardians of our moral? The Revolution gave guns to elements that could not handle even tiny problems and all hell broke loose as the hunt was declared for the young who had made the Revolution in the first place. As blood flowed on the pot-holed and sad streets and mothers wept in silence, Mesfin, the ex-bully of my street, became a Kebele chairman. He had the power over all our lives and he walked up and down our street with his

Russian gun and a new arrogant gait. Frogs were imagining themselves as elephants; rogues were given the gun and the power to shit on our heads.

He sent two of his armed guards to haul me over to the Kebele office. The jail, where I was thrown into for a few hours, was full of tortured youngsters whose festering wounds smelt foul. Blood, sweat and unwashed bodies, bad smell for sure but not as foul as the breath of the man who had raped me before I turned fourteen. I saw in the eyes of the prisoners little fear or self – pity. They were facing probable death, and most were later strangled by piano wire or shot in the dead of the night and dumped into anonymous mass graves outside the City, but they seemed to have ignored altogether the end they knew awaited them. I saw them caring for each other and they tried to comfort me also. I was quick to inform them that I deserved none of their concern or sympathy since I had done nothing heroic or worthwhile to land me in prison other than managing to survive. I must admit I was also afraid that any association with them would complicate my case.

"You have to be re-educated," Mesfin barked at me as I stood in front of his desk flanked by two armed guards. "The Revolution has come to free the likes of you. Prostitution is a vice we are going to wipe out; it is the sign of bourgeois decadence. So, no more whoring is allowed for you. You will also come here to get politically educated and we shall find respectable work for you." He went on and on but I had tuned him out altogether. He spoke like some foreign preacher and was as boring as his ugly military bosses and the revolution they had hijacked by their arms.

I had enough experience to imagine what would follow soon. On the third night of my summons to the Kebele office, Mesfin himself sneaked over to my place and slept over. Much as I detested having sex with him I was in no position to refuse, what with him being the head of the Kebele and a powerful man. He did not pay for my services but came over again and again till the shooting in the city between the government and its young enemies intensified and he stayed away fearing an ambush. At the time, many Kebele chairmen were being killed. If Mesfin did not come, others did. The temptation to sin respected no revolutionary decree. The more they thought I was a forbidden fruit, the more my countrymen flocked to my bed to be "cured" as they claimed to assuage their own guilty complex. I survived but those were really cursed times which broke families and buried many dreams in mass graves.

As I said, I survived, finding ways and means to subvert the system that declared itself beyond greed but was soon to be as rotten as a cat's carcass left on top of the garbage pile. Discretion was of course crucial, society frowned upon those strutting proudly like a peacock or doing what we call the "iyug iyug" (see me, see me). You keep a low profile, stay hidden away from the limelight and the stage, and people, who mistake caution for timidity, will appreciate you all the more. As the saying goes "iyugn iyugn debkugn yametal" those who say iyugn iyugn will soon declare "debkugn,debkugn" (hide me, hide me). I dressed in subdued colors though I liked loud colors like the traditional weavers, those gentle and kind people we used to call Dorzes. I avoided ostentation and kept my money not in a government bank but in an iron box buried under my own bed

By the time the military government collapsed from its own sins and blunders as much from assaults by its armed foes, I was someone you could call well to do in this land of poverty. I had also reached my twilight years given the average life expectancy was no more than thirty- seven. I had scant formal education as I could read and write but lots of experience. I could be called worldly and even wise. In other words, I had few illusions and I was as ever ready to sacrifice anyone or any creature-like the mouse I had torched in my young days to get what I wanted. Not that I wanted much, just acceptance, maybe a revenge on the society that had shunned me even when its male members bedded me in the dark. I actually did not know what I wanted, just lived on like millions in the country, accepting whatever fate dealt out, not expecting much, not complaining much lest a vindictive God worsened things. The new rulers came with a lot of promise just like their predecessors and it was not long before they also started to shoot at innocent youngsters. These ones came from the jungle and were as cultured and as restrained as the hyenas they must have often come across in their guerrilla hideouts. Crude and raw, they descended upon the city like an army of rapacious locusts. Deprived for long of the company of women, the soldiers jumped on anyone with or without a skirt. The first soldier who slept with me after paying me almost double my usual price beat me up when he saw my small penis though it did not prevent him from doing what he came to do in the first place. Constipated like most Northern males, he was, however, comfortable in the dark, ecstatic and even hollering, as he came, no doubt enjoying the depravity, his own shame.

One of the boys who was in the gang of Mesfin became the new Kebele head -- though we did not know it at the time, he came from the same region as our new rulers. The more things seem to change the more they remain the same; in our country, today eerily resembles yesterday. I was summoned to the Kebele and brought before the new chairman.

"You belong to the oppressor ethnic group," my old friend now told me. If he expected me to cringe I didn't. He was already sounding like Mesfin, a wound up doll, boring and mercenary. "You are what you are and you cannot prostitute yourself and spread the scourge of AIDS. Have you been tested? You are very thin you know."

He was thinner than me but I did not dare to ask him if he had the fatal disease. "I am as healthy as the other person," I replied which could also have been taken as an admission of being diseased since most of the City population had the scourge or another equally devastating disease. He did not get my hidden comment- he took me at my word. Our new rulers and their minions were all too crude and crass.

"That is good. Stay clean."

Of course, he also came the same night to have sex with me and he put on the condom only after I had insisted. I started to suspect that everyone in Mesfin's gang had actually been dreaming to land between my thighs. He was no better lover than Mesfin and by this time I was past caring about such things. He did not pay at all for my services—so what else was new?

The land was still grim and the people poorer. The new rulers lived in an opulence that became all the more grotesque because of the contrast with the pathetic existence of most of the city dwellers that had sunk to the lowest depths of poverty. Children starved and slept on the streets in the thousands. Mothers prayed to God for deliverance, for mercy and as usual God chose to sleep on his ears, unhearing and unconcerned. To avoid the measles stay far from the afflicted: I stayed aloof from the new chiefs and rulers. I kept to myself and in my old age started to go to church often though I never prayed. But trouble found me by itself. The new chairman of the Kebele had me arrested and jailed. He threatened to accuse me of belonging to the very illegal organization that the new government also hated with fury. Unless. There is always an "unless" when those in power misuse their office and press on our bent shoulders. Unless I gave him a lot of money. He was sure I had it and no amount of protest on my part could dissuade him. In the end, I agreed to pay and pay I did to stay out of prison. I admit I was cowardly but I had never found it difficult to accept my weakness. The worst coward is the one who imagines he is brave. I still had some money left but I really did not care since I had little of the things in life that really mattered. I was alone, an outsider, a godolo, someone to avoid except in the dark, in a desperate moment of devilish abandon or need. No one except my mother had ever been seen embracing me in the open, in daylight. Yet, I had to get my revenge. Odd and old they may call me but I shared many of the characteristics of my fellow City dwellers.

I went to my friend the "tenqaye", the witch doctor was now quite old but still busy and making money. Revolution or not, whores and witch doctors make a lot of money, the more their services deemed unnecessary and objectionable the more the very people who condemned them come surreptitiously and in the dark to seek their services. My friend listened to my request and promised to do what I asked within the week.

The Kebele chairman who had robbed me off my money was fast asleep in his three- roomed house (confiscated from a man called "anti-peace" and sent to the dungeons) when the "anderibi" (invisible stones) rained on his tin roof. The stones rained down on his house and he could not fathom or see who was doing the throwing. Neighbours stayed in their houses and none ventured out to help him though he was screaming and losing his head. Unable to stop the stones the man rushed into his house, got out his automatic gun and started shooting till he emptied not one but three magazines. The police and soldiers came over to arrest him on the spot. Of course, by the time they arrived the "anderibi" had stopped and there were no "invisible" stones to be seen coming down from the "heavens" to give credence to his claim that he was an "anderibi" victim. He was considered drunk or at least a victim of backward beliefs to which no modern cadre of a self declared revolutionary government should fall victim. There was also the fact that some dwellers in the same district gave testimony to the effect that the Chairman was a drunkard, a robber and abused his powers in order to give a bad image of the "good" government. A fallen tree will be struck by far too many axes, as we say. We know how to give a man a bad name and make his trip to the dungeon faster.

My money? The night they took him to jail screaming and protesting, I managed to enter his house and to search it all over. By eight in the morning, I had found more money than he had taken from me hidden, so unoriginally, inside a suitcase with a false bottom. I took my money and took the rest to the witch doctor.

"You keep it," he said refusing my offer. But I insisted. He refused. I persisted. In the end, he took it saying: "I think the boys who helped the spirits and had a sleepless night aside from tired arms will not mind sharing it among themselves."

I did not think they would. After all, had they been caught they would have been beaten and thrown into the overcrowded jails. They did a dangerous thing without any pay, to do a favor to the Tenquai, the witch doctor, and me. Maybe, you shouldn't always torch helpless creatures to get what you want. Some other children in the past harassed and hurt me while these ones took a risk to help. Maybe all was not lost, not all people were bad. It was a completely new feeling for me-maybe it was time to think of others, to do something useful for them. I must admit it felt good, better than cynical, and I hoped I would continue to feel this way at least for a day or two. No need to expect from life what it cannot deliver being as it was a burden for which I had been forced to pay. God knows I had little to thank for—I never even enjoyed a good song or a captivating book. People used me; no one except my mother ever really loved me. It had been a rough ride and a high price to pay just to be alive but I was trying to be happy enough just for getting a discount from time to time.

The Case Of The Criminal Walk

"*G*ag the prisoner," judge Hagos barked. "Chain his legs to the chair."

The policeman shifted his Ak-47 on his shoulder and proceeded to gag the frail prisoner whose wrinkled face was lit up by a mischievous smile. With the prisoner gagged by a dirty piece of cloth and chained to the chair, Judge Hagos turned his bloodshot eyes to the prosecutors' table. "Proceed," he ordered.

Judge Hagos was a thin, hog- nosed man with a cadaverous face that promised no mercy or consideration.

"The prisoner is an expert at wasting the time of the court," the prosecutor begun. A fat man with a sweaty face and a whining voice, he cast a contemptuous look towards the gagged and chained prisoner in the dock. "Five months we have been here as he procrastinates, plays with words, denies every decent accusation and daringly claims to be innocent."

The prosecutor wagged his fat finger at the prisoner and went on: "He was caught by vigilant guards jay walking outside of his Kilil while the law has clearly stipulated that no one without an official permit should be found outside of his designated region. When he was accosted and told of his crime, he committed yet another verbal assault on the government by deriding the police with 'are we in a concentration camp? Can't we move freely in our own country?' - type of diatribe. The police said he spoke with bitter resentment, his face contorted by chauvinist fury. He alleged that the government runs concentration camps while it is on record that the government has said it holds not even one political prisoner. He opposed the rules and regulations that have set up the ethnic Kilils all over Ethiopia and liberated the people to freely move inside and only inside their own region. No more will an oppressed be constrained to trek all the way to the capital here to argue a court case. It is all handled right there in his Kilil's capital except in special cases like this one.

"What are the charges actually?" asked Judge Hagos with a trace of impatience in his voice.

"Illegal crossing of Kilil borders," said the prosecutor reading from a paper. "Jay walking. Counter revolutionary declarations. Resisting arrest. Thinking anti-peace thoughts. Going against the revolutionary ethnic politics of our government. Wasting the court's time as your honor has observed. Fixing a contemptuous smile on his face on a permanent basis."

"What are you asking for?" Judge Hagos enjoyed sentencing people to long prison terms but could hardly bear the formalities of trying a case. He was of the opinion that everyone knew the cases were decided upon long before the trials begun and thus there was no need to waste time since no one was duped. But the higher ups had said this was a necessary show for the foreigners who were giving money to the Justice Ministry. Judge Hagos has suffered hunger and misery in his younger days and was not one to spit in a hard-found soup even if it had only three lentil pieces and no meat at all. And so, he tolerated the show to the best of his ability while letting the pain show on his tightly drawn and grim face.

"The State is asking the maximum on all," said the prosecutor. "A total of 76 years imprisonment with hard labor."

Judge Hagos beamed.

"Of course there are those who may snicker and say that no citizen lives that long," went on the prosecutor. "But that is not the issue. We want him in prison till he dies, no parole, no mercy."

Judge Hagos looked threateningly at the defense attorney, a small man with a haunted look on his round face.

"Call your witnesses," ordered Judge Hagos.

The first witness was sworn in.

"You are a policeman, yes?" asked the prosecutor.

The witness dressed in a police uniform said yes.

"When did you first meet the prisoner?"

"I never knew the criminal", replied the witness defensively.

The prosecutor smiled.

"I know you did not know him like you know, know a friend. You are a policeman and he a criminal. How did your paths cross?"

"Our paths did not cross," corrected the witness. "I crossed over to his side of the street and arrested him. Policeman Gebru was also with me."

"Why did you arrest him then?"

"He was walking outside of his Kilil."

"How did you know that?"

"We were told."

"By whom?"

"The security agents following him."

"Why were they following him?"

"They did not say but we assume it was because he was a criminal."

"There he was, this dangerous criminal being followed by

vigilant security agents across Kilil lines and he was, you say, walking arrogantly despite his violations of the law."

The policeman did not seem to understand what was expected of him and he kept quiet. "Where is policeman Gebru now?"

"He is sick and in the Police hospital."

"Was he driven to the hospital bed by the vile words of the prisoner?"

"He took the bus," said the policeman. "He had what they said was food poisoning."

"Aha, poison!" said the prosecutor with a tone thick with insinuation. "We shall come to that later. Why did you arrest the prisoner?"

"As I said we were told to do so?"

"But what cover did you invoke?"

"Cover?"

" I mean he was arrested for walking outside of his Kilil, wasn't he?"

"Yes."

"It is a crime to do so?"

"Yes."

"Was it a crime during the past regime?"

"No."

"And people had to walk all over Ethiopia, barefoot and with jiggers", said the prosecutor shaking his head. "We have so much to praise for today but the prisoner had to violate this humane law. What did he say when you arrested him?"

"He said he was an Ethiopian and free to walk anywhere in his country."

"Is he a sportsman?" scoffed the Prosecutor. "Does he walk for a living?"

"I heard he was a teacher."

"An idle man who wants to walk all over the country. Why didn't he run like Haile Gebre Sellasie or Kenenisa and get millions and escape poverty?"

The policeman knew the name of the athletes and he smiled.

"How was he walking?"

"What do you mean?"

"Was he strolling arrogantly? Walking briskly? Were his lips curled in disgust as he walked? Were his eyes narrow with contempt like a chuvinist? Was he pounding at the pavement or moving surreptitiously like a spy? Did he dodder, falter, lumber, stagger, totter, trudge, hobble or plod? When you saw him walk did you see an innocent man like say someone rushing to a church not to miss Mass? Or did you see a suspicious man with a saintly smile like all criminals, puffed up with arrogance, pupils dilated, happy at the mere thought of having trampled on yet another sacred law, angrily pounding on our poor road? Did he prowl, tiptoe, slink away or stalk? Was he shuffling, slouching off or creeping? Did he march, surge or meander? A lot depends on that walk."

The prosecutor wiped his sweaty face with a red handkerchief.

The witness looked confused. He said: "We did not follow him for long. I would say he was walking with a purpose?"

"To break the law of course," shouted the Prosecutor. Judge Hagos beamed-- he also liked to shout whenever he dealt with prisoners. "Let us try to pin point the criminal walk. Was it leisurely like a stroll, the pastime of a lazy man propagating unemployment? Was he moving briskly like a criminal trying to distance himself from the scene of his foul crime? Was he lifting his legs up like the parading soldiers of the former regime and pounding hard on our pavement to dig potholes? Or was he trying to be smaller than his shadow and walking stealthily? Think now!"

The witness looked up imploringly towards Judge Hagos.

"There is no way out", the Judge told him sternly. "I know you are a policeman but sometimes even you must make the effort to think."

The policeman wore his anxiety on his face and knitted his brows.

"I would say," he replied finally, "that the prisoner was walking the dangerous criminal walk. Between a stealth and a maneuver. I would even say the arrogant walk of a Kilil-hopper."

The prosecutor smiled. "The latest and most dangerous species of the grass hopper I would say. Let the records show Your Honor that the prisoner engaged in criminal cross- Kilil walking which, if let unpunished, would destroy the stay put in your own region system within a short period. The criminal walk as we all know combines the rush and the prowl with the swoop and stomp, the trudge with the swagger, and all this accompanied by the maniacal chuckle. We have seen it before with the anti peace elements who are now languishing deservedly in the labor camps. Also, didn't he say something about a concentration camp?" prodded the prosecutor turning to the witness.

"Yes. He asked us if he was a prisoner in a concentration camp?"

"And what did you law enforcers reply?"

" I said to him he could very well be in one if he violates the law."

The Prosecutor cleared his throat and said: "Meaning, of course, that it is such criminals like himself who push good governments to the dire extreme of opening such a camp."

"More or less," said the witness with a bewildered look on his face. "We actually mentioned Shoa Robit, Dedesa and Zwai to let him know we can send him there."

"Let the records show that these are places where die hard criminals are gently put on a strict diet of a bread a day and a glass of water, taught the value of working from dawn to dusk and of the correctional role played by the stick, places where criminals are patiently reeducated and then sent back to the society," corrected the Prosecutor.

The defense attorney rose next to cross- examine.

"Do you arrest all those who walk outside of their own Kilil?"

"If we did that there will be no prison enough to hold them."

"So you arrest selectively?"

"Yes."

"Who decides who gets arrested?"

"We get the orders from our superiors."

"Were you ordered to arrest the defendant?"

"Yes."

"Before you saw him walk or after?"

" He was walking as the security men told us to detain him."

"So it did not matter whether he was walking with arrogance or strolling like a lamb?"

"Does a lamb stroll?" asked the witness and the prosecutor roared in laughter.

"Let the records show that the defendant was not arrested because he walked outside of his region," said the defense lawyer.

"Objection, Your Honor," whined the Prosecutor. "The defense lawyer cannot order the register. That is my prerogative."

"Sustained," said Judge Hagos. "The prisoner could have objected but we did not get a pip from him, did we?"

The next witness called by the Prosecutor was a middle-aged man with a cherubic face and sagging jowls. He was duly sworn in.

"Could you tell the Court your profession?"

"I am a police interrogator," replied the man in a firm voice.

"How long have you worked as an interrogator?"

"Twenty- five years at least," said the man.

"A professional no doubt." The tone of admiration in the prosecutor's voice was thick enough to cut. The witness smiled satisfied.

"No petty or hardened criminal can escape your traps," added the prosecutor. "You can tell a cross eyed fly from a distance, so to speak."

"I know a lie before it is uttered," boasted the witness. "Somewhere in the eyes, the body movement, the curl of the lips."

"I will not ask you to elaborate lest criminals get informed of your technique," said the prosecutor. "Did you interrogate the prisoner?"

"Yes I did."

"What was the angle of questioning?"

"I was informed he was an anti peace counter revolutionary element who has refused to admit his guilt?"

"Have you in the past met prisoners who readily admit their guilt?"

"Will the monkey say he stinks? Few confess outright but with some prodding in the special chamber many do. Some obdurate ones take days and even weeks. It is not in our blood to confess is what I say."

Judge Hagos nodded his head in agreement. "Yet we have Father Confessors," he commented.

"Someone accustomed to begging will beg for a crumb in his dreams," said the prosecutor. "It is a matter of habit and not really to confess and atone for their sins. But," he looked at the witness and went on, "you do not anyway expect them to admit their guilt?"

"No. We want to earn our pay. What is the use of having interrogators and torture chambers if prisoners confess outright?"

"True, true," agreed the prosecutor. "But you torture gently and humanely and not like the time of the previous regime."

"Well, I did the same job back then," said the witness. "We have changed now. I took a Renewal Seminar for three weeks to understand the intricacies of humane torture that the government cadres had been practicing while they were guerrillas. For example, we do not torture them during morning hours and not also late at night. The government officials have taken away many electrical instruments to their own region and we have to rely on manual means. I tell you there is a difference."

"Did the prisoner admit that he was a counter revolutionary?"

"Will the mule say its organ is long? No. But he would

have confessed had he not been transferred to the central prison and brought to trial."

"How did the interrogation go?"

"He was prattling about his Constitutional rights but I told him I never read the said document and he was wasting his time. He admitted that he was a teacher and a member of their association. I told him that was a crime but he argued otherwise. I informed him that in my experience there has been no association without some hidden agenda. Even the Iqub and Idir associations have secret devious ends. In the end he would have admitted that he was indeed a counter revolutionary."

"Why do you say that?"

"Because he had admitted he belonged to an association. That was a start, a promising unraveling. An Ethiopian who admits he belongs to an association that is detested by the government must have many secrets he would want to reveal at the slightest prodding."

"Yet, he held out for long as you said?" The prosecutor sounded accusatory.

"You must understand our position," retorted the witness. "All our machinery taken away. We have been reduced to relying on ordinary and unimaginative beatings, tying them with plastic cords and hanging them upside down, using needles, pins and pincers. Even the old Saris wine bottle filled with sand routine is off since we do not have those special bottles. We make do with what we have."

"Still, you do a fine job," said the prosecutor warmly. "Count the number of amputees on the street and your contribution to that statistic. We all know that the government wants to be gentle with prisoners. That is why you have to resort the humane torture". The prosecutor cast a conspiratorial smile towards Judge Hagos.

"If you had the machines we may not have a prisoner left to try for the sake of decorum at least," added Judge Hagos.

"For sure," agreed the witness. "The new victims have nothing to begrudge from the veteran torture victims. We still deliver many techniques in our arsenal. They can raise their heads and proudly walk like other torture victims of the past."

"Is there a competition between the tortured?" asked the prosecutor.

"And how," replied the witness. "The victims of the military regime claim to be the special victims of real torture and try to make the new ones feel inferior. But we torture the new ones as severely as possible to give them the chance to walk with their heads high if at all they can walk that is."

"What is your conclusion as regards the prisoner?"

"Well if you don't slaughter the sheep you can't judge the meat. I would have liked to work on him some more but that was not to be. He is a resister and as we say the obdurate criminal tires the interrogator. I think he is guilty."

The defense lawyer rose.

"What is essential is that the defendant did not admit his guilt in so many words?"

"Words are expensive," said the witness. "He implied it."

"Implied how?"

"Admitted he was a member of the association?"

"Isn't the said association legal?"

"Yes, but the government does not like it."

"Is that important so long as it is legal?"

"It is really legal only if the government really likes it."

The defense lawyer looked flustered.

"No more questions," was what he preferred to say.

The next prosecution witness was a well-known medical doctor trained for years and years in the USA and Israel.

"Doctor , did you examine the prisoner? "

"Yes," said the plump doctor in a grave voice. "He underwent a battery of blood tests and psychological questions. It is a perfected system known as the Weyin Test."

"Is it not true that Weyin Test expertly determines the ethnic origin of anyone?"

"Quite true. We have tried it on the most difficult patients, those who claim to be of mixed ethnic origins or Ethiopians and successfully determined their real origin."

"Was the prisoner a native of the Kilil he was arrested in?"

"No. The blood chromosome of the Kilil dwellers did not match his. Psychological questions were also put to him and he failed thoroughly."

"Can you just cite some of these question for our education?"

"Well, we take the patients through word association. When we say Ethiopia most of those who pass the Test mention items or things that do not exist like democracy, dinosaurs, security, enough food, etc. He insisted on replying 'my country". A pseudo patriot with deep- seated chauvinist sentiments. He could come only from specific ethnic groups. It was an easy case."

The defense attorney rose hesitantly.

"Is it true that the Weyin Test is not accepted by all sectors of the medical profession?"

The witness wrinkled up his nose. "A sick man who will not recover will ask for rain in summer. There are those who cling to their misery and ignorance and refuse to accept the strides of science. Man is comfortably defined by his own ethnic genes. As we say, the origin of the horse pulls it more strongly than any rein or harness. The Weyin Test unmasks the illusion and fake identity parading as national oneness. The family, the village, the clan and ethnic origin—these matter. One country, one nation, is a fraud."

"Yet there was a creature called Ethiopian in this country, wouldn't you agree?"

"Perhaps in every poor man's home there was once a surplus of honey and butter," said the witness. "People say there was a time when every stone was actually a bread. The 'dingaye dabo' era. Now, things have changed."

After the doctor had left the witness stand without the defense attorney venturing to ask him any question, the prosecutor informed the judge he had no more witnesses. The gagged and chained prisoner was in the same state. Judge Hagos called for silence and the court was so silent that the audience heard some flies buzzing.

"The accused is here because he violated a series of penal

code articles, both written and inferred. The Prosecution has amply proved that there was a clear case of a criminal walk, the lurking, slinking and prowling that is a sure give away of bad intent. The defendant violated the stay in your own Kilil regulation and uttered counter-revolutionary words, he resisted when tortured instead of facilitating the task of the interrogator and he belonged to a dangerous association that has been often condemned by our government. Moreover, he has wasted the court's time in the last months through his antics and ridiculous claims of rights and justice. He was not sent to school to be a sophist and a dreamer. We are now living in special times when every citizen is not just lumped under one amorphous and non-descriptive label named Ethiopian. We have doctors who help us know ourselves by examining our blood. Ethnic identity and alignment on ethnic basis is as African as the tse-tse fly. The right to have our own specific identity and to define ourselves in opposition to others is a right we gained through hard struggle. The colonialists divided us into different entities and lumped us in anomalies they call countries. If the Ibos were just that instead of being called Nigerians, would we have had a Biafran war? Of course, not. Define and divide and 'each to his own Kilil' are scientific slogans. The prisoner went against science by hopping over Kilil limitations and taking the criminal walk against the sacred policy of our government. That is why he shall be helped to walk back to prison to serve a 76 years term of solitary confinement without any chance to walk or exercise. In conclusion, I must say I am pleased to note that the defense attorney did not act as a pest."

The Coward Who Hid His Eyes

*H*e used his penis like his forefathers had wielded their spears against the invading troops of Benito Mussolini. If not to kill, at least to draw blood, and, above all, to hurt as much as possible. His targets were many, his culture and history had given him more enemies than he wanted to count. Short and plump, with a nose like a parrot's beak over a perpetually pursed slit of a mouth, he was a plain man who had long ago made the conclusion, like many such men, that he was handsome and irresistible. But, long before you really got to know him, his face told you here was man who had seen the inside of the heart of the devil and liked it.

A scholarship had taken him to Germany at a time when that country was not as flooded by foreigners as now but was still more racist than he had ever imagined it would be. It was his first trip outside of the country and he had never in his life seen so many white men (shame of shames- he has been told most were uncircumcised) and women with their own peculiar smells. He had no illusion of being welcomed as a guest in a ferenji country and was not as a result very much affected by the aloofness and racism of most Germans. Born to a rich peasant family in the central part of his country, he had finished his pre-secondary schooling in a cold rural town before coming to the City as a boarding student in a strict school run by German missionaries. Let alone Germany, his own City had shocked him with its loose morals, whore-houses, intermingling of ethnic groups and what he described as sinful debauchery and lack of "sine sir'at" (code of ethics). You couldn't tell who was a "chewa lij"(the son of a nobleman) and who the son of the gebbar, the serf. Raised by a strict, traditional and religious father, he considered himself as a chosen in all aspects: looks, complexion, class, ethnic origin and intelligence. He did live for many years in the City but the City did not rub off on him, his rural accent was still intact, his value judgments still provincial, his racism towards others, whether white or black, a constant companion.

He was friends with hypocrisy and thus patronized the bars and brothels of the City and even went alone to the small kiosks, which in most cases did not have electric lights, and whose owners were extremely poor women, some of them from ethnic groups he considered inferior, almost all smelling of butter and sweat, who charged a pittance for a night of sex. He hated himself for what he admitted was 'stooping so low"(he learnt later on it was also called slumming) but he admitted to himself that he liked it. Still, he took out his hatred on the prostitutes, using their bodies as a punching bag, trying to cause them as much pain as possible. It was at this time that one of the prostitutes unknowingly paid him back in kind by asking him if he was a shewrara, a cross- eyed.

"What do you mean cross- eyed?" he had shouted at her jumping off the bed to rush to the small cracked mirror on the cracked mud wall. He looked intensely at his eyes and though the light from the candle he held in his hand was weak, he could tell, as he had suspected in the past (and refused to admit it), the woman had spoken the truth. His eyes were a little odd; he had to admit they were cross. He decided right there and then to wear dark sun- glasses and never to take it off. When a relative in the Ministry of Education (you had to have a "we" and "ge" even at that time to move anywhere, meaning either a well placed relative/wegen/ or adequate money/genzeb) got him the German scholarship and he flew to the land of the whites. His decision never to take off his dark glasses did cause him many problems but he did not budge. For him, the son of a true gentleman and a pure blooded person never went back on his vows, no matter what. He had no intention of being a disgrace to his ethnic group and to his "chewa" family and thus he stuck to his decision. In the strange land, he bought a more fashionable dark eyeglass but he never showed his eyes to anyone.

The first girl friend he had was called Ursula and she was a petite girl with full breasts. When he undressed and still kept his glasses on she had burst out laughing and he had almost slapped her except for the fear that she may leave him aroused and unsatisfied. He had wild sex with her and the fact that she screamed as he jabbed at her increased his pleasure. He used her body without any restraint and he felt as if he was taking revenge on the part of all the patriots massacred by the Italians who were, as he said to himself, not only whites but also the allies of Hitler. White was the enemy and he had its daughter under him panting and begging him for more. He used Ursula in ways that could not be told by any decent person but within a few months he had deprived her of her personality and autonomy and made her life a taste of endless pain. He had tried to get her pregnant just to cause her problems but she took her pills diligently and had frustrated his devious plan. He finally chased her off and got another one called Sybille. She gave her place to Helga; then came Gertrude followed by Anna and so on till he left the country. He was too much a hypocrite to admit that he got whosoever he got (Helga for one almost had a moustache and elephant legs) and liked the women, and that his sexual romp had nothing to do with redeeming Ethiopian honor but by shrouding it all in such a way he felt noble and compensated for his feeling of insecurity and inadequacy. His father had given him the pompous name of Sewyew, the Man, (some Ethiopian fathers try to recoup their lost manliness by giving their sons pompous or macho names), and he in turn had named his penis "Jegnaw", the patriot, and the Man often talked to the Patriot. His full name was Sewyew Tesema, the Man has been Heard, but it was not sure if "Jegnaw" did hear him.

There were many Ethiopian girls in Germany at the time but most were politically involved and he knew they would not easily accept his quirks and chauvinism. They were openly at war against "male chauvinism", the imperial regime and what they called imperialism. The mid and late sixties were political times in Germany and he played at being a progressive to get leftist German women to his bed but at heart he was a convinced reactionary and conservative who hated and feared Marxism and believed that all Communists will end up by confiscating the land of his father or by nationalizing other people's sisters and wives. He had also seen the face of real socialism when he crossed often into East Germany as a visitor—mainly to buy Russian Vodka on the cheap-- and he had instantly hated the eerie and depressive atmosphere of East Berlin. Though all German police were for him one bundle of incorrigible racists, the grim and dour- faced police of East Germany particularly affected him. During one vacation period, he took the train and visited Italy and France, to see the ancient and beautiful cities of Rome and Paris. He used the occasion to, as he put it, "taste" French and Italian girls but none were willing to spend time with a brown parrot- like man who looked sinister in his dark glasses. Needless to say he couldn't at all understand why and how the whites, the dough-looking softies, could look down upon him, the perfect brown and beautiful Ethiopian who never mingled with the black Negroes. If only the Germans knew how I look down at these monkey- eating and worm devouring, thick- lipped Africans, he had often said to himself. But, he remained black for the whites and the Germans treated him like they treat any kinky haired "schwarz". He found the Italians warmer as a people than the haughty French who were at the time crazy enough to try to end the rule of the one leader he had considered dignified and great, De Gaulle. To tell the truth, he did not like the whites at all.

Nineteen sixty- eight and the revolutionary fervor that was gripping the youth all over the world left him cold. As he detested all public manifestations of any type of passion and emotions as "kilet" (losing face) and unworthy of a cool well-bred man like himself, he did not mix with the other Ethiopian students who were loudly demonstrating against the imperial regime. Needless to say, he considered himself too intelligent to be political and as a consequence, at least in his view, to stoop down to be mundane and ordinary. He never considered himself one of the masses or akin to the serfs—his father had serfs and his great grandfather had owned several slaves. Given the chance most Ethiopians will be glad to see back the slave system, he had concluded long ago. His heart did not beat for the downtrodden and he shed no tears for the impoverished. The wealthy have their riches and the poor their misery, all preordained, and he also believed that everyone had a destiny decided by God and we live out the script written by Him, no line or chapter changed. He scoffed at the radicals who were talking what he considered gibberish, and they called Marxism, but he was again cautious enough not to express his views in public as silence never rusts and words are like ghosts and have the bad habit of coming back to haunt the one who had uttered them. He played at being a radical when it served his purpose but he was not naïve enough to be a True Believer and to burn his bridges. He kept close contact with the Ethiopian embassy in Bonn and attended the yearly bash for the Emperor's birthday in July. He believed he was smart and far-sighted. What others would call cowardice he named caution, his opportunism was presented as tact and his tendency to be servile as politeness and good upbringing. Call any wild bird a hen and you can eat it with a relish, as his forefathers had said.

He did not rush back to Ethiopia when the Revolution that ended the rule of the Emperor exploded and caught by surprise even those who had been expecting it, and the Emperor was unceremoniously dumped into prison and suffocated to death by a pillow held by a junior army officer obeying other ruthless military men. He went back only after the sound of gunfire had died in the City and towns. The new military regime had been battling against a determined Opposition that had managed to have popular support. In the City and the towns, the government's so called Red Terror was in full swing and the Opposition was also shooting back though the outcome was a foregone conclusion given the fact that the government was enjoying support from the Soviet super power. As the gunfire subsided and the Terror achieved its murderous objectives, the government turned against its own intellectual allies and slaughtered them in their turn.

It was then that his time had come to go back. There was a big playing field and it was empty as most of the qualified intellectuals had been killed, jailed or forced into hiding or exile. He flew Ethiopian Air Lines from Frankfurt and landed on the City with the determination to be a "Somebody" soon enough. All the old neighborhoods and kiosks were there, just more dilapidated, and the people as a whole looked more anxious and crushed by their fears and traumas. There was too much despair in the air but he was totally unmoved by the change to the worst. And it did not take him long to fit in as he was a man with his priorities set in black and white. Since those in power were allied to the Soviets and claiming to be Communists- he had prepared himself by reading not the boring volumes but the abridged editions and selected quotations of the Marxist books and was able to present himself as worthy material fit to be a cadre or an ideologue. Revolutionary rhetoric is not that difficult to learn and he had memorized it all in a very short time. More importantly, he knew that nothing endeared you to those in power as sharing the same prejudices and hatred and in a jiffy the regime's enemies became his. Publicly and vociferously, he condemned anarchists, feudalists, imperialists, secessionists and the regimes in Mogadishou and Khartoum. His passionate fulminations against the Arabs, their petrodollars and the CIA were pure gems. And it had worked. Too bad if his father's rural land got nationalized-- he had had his time, Sewyew reasoned. Tesema, his father, did not recover from the loss of his land and the collapse of the imperial regime and had died shortly after the military regime assumed power. Sewyew did not go to the funeral, did not send condolences to his old mother, he did not acknowledge family at all. There was no need to identify oneself as the son of a Kulak, the new word he had learnt to describe rich peasants like his father. Wasn't love banal and loyalty a refuge for fools with no capacity to get along, adjust, or to move with the times?

He still wore his dark glasses everywhere and still used his organ as a weapon to hurt and humiliate women but this did not affect his rise up the bureaucratic ladder. He spoke English and German as foreign languages and spoke none of the local ones other than his mother tongue. A relative introduced him to a well-placed Colonel who in turn introduced him to a civilian power broker close to the Chairman and absolute master of the whole country and soon enough he was made a deputy in the European Department of the Foreign Ministry with special assignment to focus on Germany. There was cut throat competition in the bureaucracy as all power was concentrated in the hands of the supreme dictator and his few top advisors while all others were out in the cold, vulnerable. Getting the right ears was the name of the game, a make or break issue, life or death. His own ears were big and protruding out like satellite dishes from his head. He used them well, like radars tuned and ready to intercept all rumors and information, nothing salacious escaping, all retrieved, picked and whisked in. The right information and rumor was whispered to the right official who would be grateful in due course of time. If someone had told him he was a simple informer and rumor merchant he would have had a hard time accepting it. He believed he was doing the right thing to protect himself and to guarantee his future. To get to the top of the ladder first it was not enough to move faster but one must also kick and shove aside all others.

His boss was a military man who had got the job because he had shined during the bloody purges by personally dispatching countless enemies of the 'Great Chairman." He had no experience at all in the diplomatic field and hardly knew anything on any of the countries of Europe he was assigned to handle. And here was where he came in useful as the deputy. He did all the work and let the boss claim the credit and thus gained his praise and confidence. It was not long before the boss became totally dependent on him and when the right time came Sewyew advised him to seek an ambassadorial post in Europe. "Better to meet great leaders and ambassadors rather than stay behind a desk here. Your talents need a bigger field. Go foreign." The military man, with an enormous ego like most uncouth military officers, lapped it up and it was not long before he had begged the Chairman to be sent as ambassador to a west European country. When he was dispatched to Rome, Sewyew became the head of the European Department within the Foreign Ministry and set his eyes on the ministerial posts.

Yet, he never became a minister and did not go any higher than the post of department head. He survived by exercising caution and considering each and every day as an aptitude test. He had of course his models, individuals who had held high posts during the time of the Emperor and continued to be top officials under the military. He observed them, studied their declarations and collected all information pertaining to them. He realized it was all a question of timing backed by a total lack of scruples and self- respect. They had bent so low so often as to soil their coat lapels permanently but it had no nasty smell for them. They had betrayed so many friends that they had long ago stopped smelling foul from treason. The trick was also to never say no to any humiliating posting. Minister today, director tomorrow, deputy governor in a remote rural outpost the next time…. they said thank you and took it and waited. Furthermore, when the heat and intrigue at the Court (imperial or Red it did not change) increased, they had all the knack to be inconspicuous, to shrink, to retreat to the background and let the fire consume its foolish victims and to give time for the wrath of the tyrant to cool down before they resurfaced, to be seen, to be noticed and to say "we are here for any appointment, venerable leader". The right time and the right place—that was the art. Like the wise reed which bends to let the flood pass and to rise again, ever present, flexible, unbroken. "Alena", here we are, the slogan of all survivors. It was very much like Judo, no resistance to a direct and contrary force but using the momentum for your gain. Sewyew tried to learn and apply but he had a lot of handicaps to remove. He did try though.

To get respectability and also strike a good connection he married a "spinsterish" and plain- looking daughter of a Colonel reputed to be close to the ruler of the country. The Colonel was purged two years later but by that time Sewyew's wife had given birth to a son and a daughter and he could not divorce her lest the bigwigs, who did divorce their own wives, look at that negatively. (Hypocrisy! hypocrisy! It was a society more concerned with saving face rather than living a decent life). He also did not have the right political background that he could whip out at every opportunity ("I was a top militant of the student movement, a leftist activist during the outbreak of the Revolution and a member of………….afterwards, etc."), and so he had opted for the next best thing: he went on a six months course to study international diplomacy in Sofia, Soviet-camp Bulgaria.

When he returned, he still went to his whores, discreetly, and he never missed the chance to go to the kiosks and cheap sex outlets. It was his weakness and his secret. He kept his glasses on all the time, everywhere, and since his superiors had assumed that one of his eyes may be blinded and ugly to look at none had pressed him to take the glasses off. Which was all the best for him. He beat his wife from time to time just to pay her back for her father's inability to avoid being purged. If he hadn't loved her at first he hated her lividly in the process and made her life miserable and, as a consequence, he felt like many other such husbands, quite comfortable. He knew she was too scared to get a lover and she was forced, like many other women, to take out her frustration by throwing herself into religion and going to the church everyday.

And then one day he was summoned to the office of the Foreign Minister.

"Your record has been very good," said the plump Minister after offering him coffee. "The Revolution needs more people like you."

Sewyew flashed what he imagined to be a neutral smile.

The Minister went on: "As you know, our enemies are getting stronger thanks to the help of Arab petrodollar and imperialism. We are forced to buy time, the people are spineless and not giving us enough recruits for the army and the militia. We therefore have to negotiate. One step back, two steps foreword as the great Marx had said."

Sewyew nodded in assent though he remembered the phrase or something like it actually belonged to Lenin.

"You have been chosen to be a part of the negotiating delegation to go to Rome. It is a very important duty, an honor which shows the Revolution trusts you."

"I am moved beyond words,' said Sewyew resorting to the dry words and cliché favored at the time. "My life belongs to the Revolution. I will try to be up to the job and the trust shown to me."

And thus he left for Rome together with a civilian ideologue, one of the gang of four close to the Chairman himself, who never smiled and had been given the popular nickname "kulf qit" ("padlocked-anus"), as intense constipation was deemed responsible for his tightly drawn and pained features. His deputy was a military officer from the Chairman's office, an oily fat man who was mainly going to Rome to buy shoes and clothes for his family and mistresses. Sewyew was named political advisor to the twelve- man delegation. In Rome, the negotiations between two irrational and hard line camps were boring, long and leading nowhere but it was a city he had liked and he was determined to have a good time. One evening he was all by himself in the plush hotel bar hoping to pick an Italian woman (whore or nun he did not care) when a white man had approached him and struck a conversation with him in German. The man seemed to know all the places frequented by Sewyew in Germany. Over drinks, they talked a lot about Germany, racism, and Africa's problems, politics at large and about women too. Sewyew found the conversation relaxing and they made an appointment to meet the next day in the man's room for "quiet boozing and talk."

Sewyew did not know that this same strange drinking partner of his, who claimed to be German, was actually an American and the same experienced intelligence operative who had recruited in the past many notorious agents who had betrayed their country for money and personal gain. Sewyew was an ideal candidate, he had no scruples, very faint patriotism, and even though he believed he did not like Western countries he did love money and power. They had studied him well. On their fourth meeting, the white man offered good rewards though he was cautious enough to couch the whole offer in generalities, shared causes, common faith to defend against the Godless, time to save the proud and ancient country, be part of the valiant soldiers who fight in the dark. Sewyew was not a romantic and was thus not particularly attracted by any allusion to a sacred mission (he read not many books but had long ago found the few adventure and romantic novels he had read boring) but he was glad that the man was indirect and had helped him to save face. He became a spy and found out nothing really changed except that he was getting more money and passing information to his contact man in Addis Abeba, a Consul in the Spanish embassy. He had no doubt that the secessionists were subsequently informed by the Americans on the negotiating strategy of the government but Sewyew knew that it was a sinking ship, this moribund military regime, and he had absolutely no intention of sacrificing his future. If someone had told him that he was now the white man's slave and that he could be taken as a traitor to his country he would have laughed loud at such naivety—he had no country to betray, his loyalty was to himself and he came first and foremost. The sad thing was that Sewyew was fast becoming the typical intellectual of the hapless country.

And the future came in 1991 in the form of a brief fight to take the City which had already been rendered defenseless by her presumed defenders who had received orders from their Washington pay masters and demobilized the soldiers to prepare an easy takeover by the rebels. The rebels marched in without much of a fight but not to public acclamation. Students (always students!) demonstrated against their arrival and the rebels shot several of the young and unarmed students dead and marched into the palace. Sewyew, who cautiously stayed in doors but followed the news over the radio (specially the VOA and the BBC), knew now for sure that little had changed. A government that pulls the trigger the moment some youngsters march in a noisy but peaceful demonstration against it was as Ethiopian as he had ever known one to be. The decisive use of force, the penchant for drastic action, the threatening official statements over the local radio and the ignorance of the guerrillas all seemed to him heaven sent. He felt there was still a lot of need for his kind, the jokers, the crooked nails for every crooked hole. Yet, the fact that other secret employees of the Americans had to flee or hide in some foreign embassies did not give him much assurance. Spies and informers, he knew, were expendable in poor countries, yet he did not lose hope.

The new government called on all officials, civilian and military, to report to a designated place. Sewyew went dutifully and surprised himself by feeling sad at the sight of Generals and Colonels, party leaders and big-shots, queuing up to report to armed peasant youngsters whose outward arrogance barely hid their amazement at the whole turn of events and the bigness and novelty of the City itself. Sewyew got registered and was told that he would be contacted, not to leave town. Military officers, high- level security and police personnel and high executives of the defunct ruling party were all rounded up and sent to reeducation camps. Sewyew was not called. He started going out of his house, taking long walks in the noisy Piazza and Mercato, noticing the huge crowds, the heat, the dust, the smell of spices intermingled with the stink of exposed sewage, observing the depth of stifling poverty all around, pushing away the hordes of beggars, young and old, the maimed and bleeding, the demobilized soldiers shamelessly exposing their medals of courage as they begged, the sick and smelly who came to him like the army of fleas in the Zuquala monastery he had visited in his young days. He did wonder at the resilience and patience of the people but he was quick to conclude that they were fatalists accepting any burden dumped on them and deluding themselves through a possible heavenly reward. Many of the people on the streets were deformed, diseased, ugly or, worse still, hopeless and crushed by their worries and fears and, he was certain, that almost all would claim to believe in God. He thought this was an excuse for their lazy despair and cowardice, for their immobility, inaction and incapacity to change their own miserable fate even if change it they couldn't. He did not modify his long held views, oh no. Fundamental opinions do not change just because an upheaval became haughty enough to call itself a Revolution. He still thought that the masses were destined to suffer-- they were cursed at birth, and anyways accustomed to their misery.

Does the ox find its horn heavy? Does the hyena refuse to devour the donkey? Will the slave who is used to his condition opt for freedom and insecurity just because some foreign educated intellectuals whisper to him abstract words of liberty? He was convinced that slaves in Ethiopia would have hanged any Spartacus themselves.

Yet, the sudden fall of the former officials who had had absolute power on the fate of millions had touched him, seeing them practically shriveled and rendered small by their defeat, all arrogant air taken out of them much like a pierced balloon, has made him somewhat sad. To each his turn was his standing belief as these were criminals in their own right, but he continued to hope that when his time came he would not suffer unduly. He restarted visiting the kiosks in the night, knowing that though his pocket were now full of condoms he was taking more than the usual risk because the AIDS scourge was spreading like a "seded isat" or a prairie fire. He started to be offended by the natural smell of the women he slept with and distantly noted that his Jegnaw was also starting to get tired of it all.

The new government was based on ethnicity and that put Sewyew at a disadvantage since he hailed from the ethnic group designated more or less as the enemy by the new masters. To his delight, however, all was not lost ("do not the courageous man and smoke always find a way out?") since some members of his own ethnic group were allied to the new masters from the north and were gathered in an official group controlled by the ruling cabal. The population, which did not hide its distaste for the barbarians from the jungle, referred to this group rather derisively as "condoms" of the ruling party. Sewyew was not perturbed by this—wasn't the condom saving lives in these terrible days? Moreover, he did not feel defeated nor was he disturbed by the ethnic chauvinism of the rulers. Cry and fulminate they may till they get tired, he said to himself, but superiority belongs to us by nature. Thus, he looked down on those who claimed to be the masters of his destiny, he laughed internally at their lack of sophistication, at their provincialism, their crudeness and he enjoyed their apparent inferiority complex. It was an uneducated lot, uncultured except in the wielding of the gun, just hurrying to eat in turn. Their home region was arid, the majority dirt-poor and always victimized by drought and, he was convinced, they even ate locusts though they claimed to be Christians. His own chauvinism was the shield he used to render theirs impotent. Hurrying to eat in turn, that's all-- he knew their greed and thereby their ruthlessness. What was power but the chance and means of eating to one's satisfaction? Sewyew knew they would taste, like what they chewed on and strive to get the time to stay in power till they swallow what they had in their mouths and bite some more. This would inevitably call for the repression as there was no way the majority would accept to serve the minority and stand aside and watch as they feasted on what did not even belong to them. A repressive government is an isolated one, Sewyew knew, vulnerable and frightened it sees enemies where even friends cast shadows. In other words, a government that would be in need of the services of Sewyew. A cat may turn into a strict and fasting monk but it will never forget its nature and ignore the milk, as the saying goes. They would call for him, they would release the torturers and killers they had arrested in moments of fervor and populism and employ them again for their own safety and survival. Can the Ethiopian change his color or the leopard his spots?

Sewyew exuded confidence and calm on the outside but he did not hide his anxiety to himself. Somehow, his instincts warned him that the new masters were more unpredictable and sadistically prone to arbitrary violence. He used all his contacts and dispatched his two children to the care of a relative living in Ohio, USA. His wife left the City and went to her aunts in the Debre Libanos area where the famous monastery would be close to her. It was as good as a divorce but the word was never raised or mentioned by either of the two. Alone with his intrigues and memories, he charted his plan and started the campaign to ingratiate himself to the new rulers. He attended all political meetings called by the new masters or the groups allied to them. He applied to join the group ostensibly set up to cater for his ethnic group. He was accepted immediately as his well prepared CV must have impressed the inexperienced and scantily educated cadres and chiefs who were at best just horrid propagandists. But, as he knew very well, there was no punishment for stupidity.

Appointment to posts followed ethnic quotas, and with the top and decisive posts held by the Northerners, others were distributed haphazardly to the so-called "allied groups" and 'friendly forces". His group got its share and he was recalled to the Ministry of Foreign Affairs, made again the head of the European desk. His spy- masters renewed their contact with him, paid him more (the inflation counts) and this time he was reporting to an Arab teacher at the University where the Ethiopian professors had been unceremoniously purged because they did not belong to the ethnic group of the power holders. Sewyew was satisfied with himself, satisfied just, for he never defined himself as happy, no. Only drunks and fools imagined themselves happy and he considered himself to be neither of the two.

The Minister was a spectacled and colorless man whose assumed reserve hid an astonishing degree of inexperience and insecurity. He was taciturn because he had little to say, he listened to his minions and picked the opinion he liked the most to determine policy. Not that he had the power to decide on all issues. Once again, the main rein was held by a dwarfish street smart dictator, who was called the goat by the people behind his back, always behind his back for, even if there was no emperor on the throne, lése majestè was alive. Sewyew surmised that the Minister was a good candidate for ego stroking and he went at it with vigor, efficiency and determination. His only obstacle was the deputy minister who had served the fallen regime and had somehow managed to survive and stay on top. An able survivor, Sewyew had to admit with admiration, and most probably a potential enemy who had to be neutralized. What was his weak point? His secret? Everyone who was someone had his own secret or believed he had one to give worth to his existence and place in society. Most of the times, the Ethiopian was his own worst enemy, no one was beyond reproach, the whole country was awash with skeletons in mass graves and closets. A man with a secret was but a vulnerable man. Dig, Sewyew ordered himself.

But the main task was to ingratiate himself with the Minister and this he was able to do within a short six months period, so much so that the Minister took him along on all his trips not only to Europe but to Africa and the USA too. Sewyew became a confidante and a sort of a friend, even procuring women for the Minister (who claimed his wife had turned frigid and was interested only in money), staying up till dawn drinking Black Label Johnny Walker and, sometimes, even the more expensive Blue Label one, picking gossips and information from the tipsy and drunk Minister. Some of this he passed to his American employers, others he kept for himself, to use when the right occasion presented itself. He also went to the right bars frequented by the powerful elite, bars opened by Ethiopians who had returned from the USA and Europe mostly, bars with supposedly trendy and chic foreign names like Casablanca, Le Parisien, After Hours, Ben's Piano Bar (with no piano in sight), New York on the Kebena, La Notte Lunga, Out and In, 24 and Paradiso, bars in which the clientele spoke only American or British English after ten o'clock and where only the very, very expensive drinks were stocked in the bar. "Class, buddy, class". Here, the ethnic elite, the powerful and their minions drank themselves to stupor with high- level civil servants from other ethnic groups. Later, the Sheraton was opened, grotesque in its luxury amidst the smelly and flea-ridden slums and he started frequenting its exclusive Gaslight club, following the elite who congregated there almost every night. He hated caviar but had learnt to eat some to blend in with the high society. The security at the Sheraton was tighter than a starving man's belt and it helped him feel part of the scared powerful. He could not go often as it was expensive and he did not have the free food and drink pass given for six months (renewable) to the high officials by the owner of the Hotel. In short, he was doing what was referred to as having one's face beaten, in other words diligently exposing himself to the notice and attention of the powerful, sort of being "in their sight, in their mind".

What would have been a boring and routine story of an unscrupulous opportunist turned as interesting as the fate of the fast disappearing Red Fox of the Semien and Bale mountains when Sewyew got arrested though he had no one close to him to notice it.

Calamities come so often, drought and famine are so common and death is so pervasive that tragedy is in-built in the very soul of the Ethiopian. A born coward, and thereby an able opportunist, Sewyew was scared when the police came for him and when he was taken into a walled compound (which he suspected was one of the ghost prisons) and thrown into a dark room. It was like being dumped into a toilet hole. He vomited outright, perhaps more from fear than from the overpowering nasty smell. It was a heaving and painful act that led him to tears. They had taken away his eyeglasses, trousers, shirt and jacket and he was just in his underclothes and did not have a handkerchief to wipe himself with. He used his under shirt as a towel. His bare soles on the cold cement floor made him bend. He groped for the wall and slid down to the floor to sit and sob. He was by himself, in total darkness, alone with his fear and shame and the foul smell now supplemented by the acid odor of his sweaty armpits. It felt as if he was in a coffin, in a grave but alive to appreciate the terror. He shuddered and hugged his knees close and listened to his own sobs that went on uncomforted by anyone.

He who eats alone dies alone, say Ethiopians, perpetual victims of famine and of official greed. Sewyew was alone in the dungeon because he had been alone in life but this was not foremost in his mind at the time. He was trying to cover his tracks, to seek where he had made the faux pas, the reason for his landing in jail. The brutal opening of the door of the cell interrupted his search and a thin and gaunt man in civilian clothes ordered him out. He had said "wita!" (come out) with a northern accent. Sewyew's heart missed a beat. He went out into a dimly lighted corridor. "Quetil!", ("move!"), the man ordered and Sewyew dragged himself hesitantly towards the door at the far end to which the man had pointed. When they reached the door, the man passed Sewyew, opened the door and dragged Sewyew in. He went out and closed the door behind Sewyew who stumbled in, into a room lit by a naked bulb hanging from the roof. There was a metal chair fixed to the floor in the middle of the room that had the offensive smell of a dirty latrine and cheap cigarettes. There were two thin men in shirt- sleeves in the room, sitting at the left corner, near a long table full of instruments.

"Sit!" ordered one of the men pointing at the metal chair. A shaking Sewyew moved in and complied. The other man came over and strapped Sewyew to the chair.

"You are the big man trying to damage our government," he sneered.

Sewyew was about to speak when a vicious slap knocked him back. "Speak when you are spoken too, you understand." Tears flowed down Sewyew's cheeks.

The two men brought their chairs close to his and one of them went back to the big table and picked up some instruments that he carried over. As he approached, Sewyew noted that the man was holding knives, a pincer, a lighter, several long needles and a hammer. The man put the instruments on the floor. They sat flanking him. One of the men smelt like a goat, Sewyew noticed despite his terror. He was ready to confess to mass murder.

"Do you deny or admit your guilt?" one of the men asked.

"Why should he?" the other man said in a mocking voice. "An intellectual, isn't he? He can always dupe us, won't he?"

Sewyew had not even seen the other man pick the hammer but the hard blow to his kneecap made him scream with pain.

"The baby cries," said the man with the hammer. "And we have not even begun."

"What have I done to deserve this?" Sewyew managed to wail as his whole body convulsed with acute pain.

"Probably nothing," said the other thin man as he stabbed the naked thigh of Sewyew with a sharp and long needle, drawing blood and screams from the victim.

The other man lit a cigarette. "Why do you need to be guilty to be tortured?" he said as he blew out smoke.

"Why do they always waste time with guilt and innocence?" the other one said. "They commit so many crimes that they are always candidates. They only had to avoid being caught."

The other torturer nodded and put out the cigarette on Sewyew's other thigh. Sewyew was screaming with pain and he did not even realize he had wetted himself until the other one said aloud, "already pissing? Let us see who is doing that?" and the man pulled down Sewyew's wet underwear and yanked out the shrinking Jegnaw out.

"How many crimes have you committed with this stupid little thing?"

The long needle came down on Jegnaw and Sewyew fainted. The two men looked at one another and shrugged.

"What is he in for anyway?" asked the younger one.

"They did not say," the other one replied. "They just said give him the treatment for a day or two."

"You think he can endure?"

"He will. They are too scared to die. I know his type."

"Do they want to interrogate him?"

"I wouldn't know," said the other man. "Few of the ones we have in the cells have been really interrogated. They bring them for us and they forget them in the dark cells."

They both knew that in one dark room in this same villa there were at least six prisoners who had been kept there for the past four years.

They slapped Sewyew back to consciousness and gave him the whole treatment till he fainted again. All the while, as they tortured him and he screamed in pain, the two men continued to talk of their weekend adventures with whores and street girls. They were laughing loudly at their own jokes when he had fainted from the pincer to the calf treatment.

Sewyew awoke in the dark and smelly room he considered to have been his previous cell. His whole body ached and his lips were swollen, his thighs burnt by cigarettes and lighters throbbing, his calf flesh torn off. The kneecap and his Jegnaw sent excruciating pain all over his body. He was flat on his back and as he tried to sit up he shrieked in pain. He stayed where he was and this time he was conscious as he peed on himself. The cement floor was colder than before and he imagined night must have fallen. While his bodily pain occupied his attention he was still desperately trying to find out where he hade made the wrong step. He passed a sleepless night, a tortured man he did not even once think of all the valiant young men and women who had, before him, suffered such pain and more. Alien to solidarity and forever alone, and thus vulnerable, his one night of torture was all the more painful and unbearable to him.

The next day, he was dragged back to the torture room and beaten all over again. The room stank of his blood, of sweat and fear. They threw him back into his dark room and it was long after that he could drag himself to one dark corner of the room, lean on the wall and relieve himself. He painfully dragged himself away from the spot and went to another corner. Three times they came for him all in all and three times he was tortured by the bored men who talked of women, drinks, the price of sugar and of people they knew who had died of AIDS as they totally ignored his screams while calmly mutilating his body.

On the third day, they gave him small dry bread with a glass of water. On the fourth day, he was not tortured. The fifth too he was given bread and water but left alone with his regrets and devastated body. On the sixth day, the guards took him into a room that was obviously a well-furnished office. His whole body ached. The elderly man sitting behind the mahogany desk was dressed in a dark woolen suit, white shirt and red tie. He seemed out of place in the prison and torture villa. He was an ordinary looking man, Sewyew observed, ordinary in that his own particularities, if any, had long ago disappeared. He could have passed as a coolie, a professor, a civil servant or a military officer, Sewyew sat in front of the man across the desk as ordered. The man grimaced and curled up his nose as the foul smell emanating from Sewyew assaulted his snub nose.

"I hope you have recovered," said the man with a smile. "Being a 'Mengist', a State, is so complicated."

Sewyew was too scared and in pain to speak. Actually he wouldn't have even if he had been able to speak: you don't show your wound to flies. The man opened a thick file and leafed through it. "It says here you have been working against the government. Dangerous activity, don't you agree? We cannot let you have a go at it. The State has to protect itself, as you very well know. You agree, don't you?"

Sewyew rose to the occasion. Maybe there was an opening, a chance; some way out. He almost forgot his pain.

"I agree completely, Sir," he replied with a voice that he hoped expressed his servility and expectations. "I have never condoned anarchy or sedition." A child suckling at his mother's breast does not wail and Sewyew was ready to please.

"That's exactly my point," said the man. "I worked in department 06 during the struggle. You know 06? Intelligence and Elimination, we had to deal with a lot of saboteurs and dissenters who would have destroyed the iron discipline needed for victory. Torture and liquidation were essential and, alas, they are still unavoidable. We cannot let dissenters run amok. Look at what happened to the Soviet Union and the whole of Eastern Europe. People are naturally envious and greedy, they all want someone else's seat or property and they are born counter revolutionaries. Many have grudges and we cannot lend a gun to someone with a grudge, can we?"

Sewyew nodded in agreement. "I know I am human and weak," he begun imploringly, "and liable to commit an offense without meaning to. But I have to say I could not fathom at all what I am specially accused of?"

"Of trying to sabotage the government."

"Sabotage?"

"Yes," said the man taking out a paper from the file. "Of being a member of an outlawed organization, of spreading negative rumors on the Prime Minister, of publicly spreading derision on the ministers of the government, of constantly reading the newspapers which attack the government, of chauvinism. The list is long I see."

"But all this is not true," Sewyew wailed. "I am a loyal member ", he said mentioning he name of the group aligned to the northerners' ruling party. "I have never uttered one negative word, I have not even had one negative thought, as God is my witness, concerning our revered Prime Minister whose intelligence has always awed me. And following the declaration of the Prime minister I never wasted time to read newspapers."

"Not even government ones?"

"Of course I read the government press. Who wouldn't?"

"I know many who don't," said the official with a mocking smile. Sewyew, sensing a trap, remained quiet.

"Didn't you say our leaders are well groomed, perfumed and regal but they talk like infants and their flowery speeches convey nothing of significance?"

"I have never uttered such nonsense," Sewyew protested.

"Didn't you call the Minister of Information an ordinary slogan weaver?"

"Never."

"You never said the Minister of Women's Affairs was a man in disguise?"

"How could I? I know she is a woman."

"You never referred to our ambassador to the UN as a short- legged camel in three piece suits."

"I never did call him that."

"So, you deny all?"

"Not all. Only the things I did not say or commit."

"You are not guilty then?"

"Who am I to conclude in such a manner?"

"Can you imagine what your guilt is?"

Sewyew just looked at the official, saying nothing.

"At this rate, I am afraid you would even deny you are Sewneh Tadele?"

"I deny it," said Sewyew.

The official looked startled. "You are not Sewneh Tadele?"

"No. I am Sewyew Tesema."

The official picked up a phone and dialed a number.

"Get me Tekle," he barked.

After a while he spoke again. "Tekle? Yes, it's me. How come I have here Sewyew Tesema when the order was given to bring in Sewneh Tadele? Yes, he has been with us almost a week. What do you mean the arresting officers made a mistake? I don't care if you send them to the jungles of Gamo Gofa as a punishment. How are we to excuse ourselves for the mistake? We cannot treat honest officials like this. The Deputy Minister? He sent them to Sewyew?"

After some minutes, the official put down the phone on its cradle. He had put on a sad face now and he shook his head slowly from right to left.

"What can I say, Ato Sewyew? A shameful and stupid mistake has been made. They were ordered to bring in Sewneh Tadele from the African desk. He is detained now by the way." Sewyew knew the man but did not feel sorry for him. "The deputy minister directed the Security men to your office. He made the mistake it seems. Sad, but there is nothing we can do. You shall be compensated, of course and there is no need to talk about what has happened here. Let it be our secret, the least you can do for our government."

Sewyew managed a smile. "Of course," he said. The damned Deputy Minister! I will get you, he vowed to himself.

"Take a week or two off and then go back to your work," the official said. "All will be arranged."

After Sewyew had been taken out of the room, washed, dressed and covered with his dark eyeglass to be driven to a clinic, the prison official rose from his chair, left his office and walked to the floor above and into a big office. A sullen-looking man was sitting on a black sofa behind a shining black mahogany table.

"All done," reported the official. "I told him it was a mistake and that the deputy minister had fingered him."

"And he will now have his grudge against the man," said the sullen man in a raspy voice.

"Which we can use. They are both from…." The official mentioned the nemesis ethnic group. "Divide and rule. Give a gun to man with a grudge is what I say. They outnumber us and we have to use all means to stay on top."

"Did he buy the whole 'we made a mistake' story?"

"He lapped it up. They want to believe, they are desperate to please. As they say, know the animal and you will know the man. They are like dogs. Beat them but throw them some bones and they will forget the humiliation. The politics of the stomach, the belly is all."

The system of picking up such officials like Sewyew and torturing them for a few days and then releasing them with profuse apologies and promises of reward was concocted by the Prime Minister himself and was being applied selectively all over the country. It was like breaking in horses and it was a clever way of pitting one official against another. The Prime Minster claimed he was a disciple of Machiavelli, like the late Emperor Haile Sellasie, though no one knew when he had read him since he had publicly asserted he hated reading and preferred talking to the president of a tiny neighboring country who was "more wise than books".

Two weeks later Sewyew returned to his office, treated for his wounds, rested and chastised but all the more wise. The moment he arrived at his office, the Deputy- Minister summoned him.

"I am glad all is settled," said the deputy minister. "I could not really tell what was the problem. They came and took Sewneh also."

"They wanted to ask me some questions," Sewyew said.

"Routine actually."

"What kind of question?" The deputy minister tried to sound uninterested but Sewyew detected the undertone of anxiety.

"You know I am loyal to you, sir," Sewyew plunged in, "I owe you a lot."

"Oh, you are a capable official, that's all," said the deputy minister with a fake smile. Sewyew knew that the man was a refined opportunist and a serpent in human form. A kindred soul, it took one to know one.

"They wanted to know about you," Sewyew said softly. "They did tell me, no they warned me, not to say anything to you but I have to tell you come what may."

"Thank you, thank you,' said the visibly shaken deputy minister. "What did they want to know? What did they ask?"

Sewyew took his time and let tears cover his eyes. He was angry enough to cry and in such situations the tears are not scarce. He took out a handkerchief and wiped his eyes. "They tortured me for six days," he lied. He stood up suddenly and moving to the side of the table pulled up his trouser and showed the deputy minister the bruised kneecaps, calves and thighs. He went back to his chair noting the shock on the deputy minister's face. As pulling out his bruised Jegnaw for inspection would have been rude and also carelessness on his part since it would have exposed his weak point, Sewyew did not show his bruised penis to the minister. Insult a foolish man in private and he will insult himself a hundred times recounting it in public—Sewyew was not foolish enough to get hurt again.

"It was horrible. They did things to me I cannot mention even to you, my close friend," Sewyew went on with a dramatic voice. "You know the deputy minister has contacts with the Opposition, they repeatedly said. You know, tell us. Accuse him and the torture will stop, they promised me. I refused. I told them you were loyal, that you hated the Opposition, that you served diligently, and so on. In the end, they had to admit that they had made a mistake. I was so convincing."

Sewyew felt like the thief who said "if they see me I will laugh it off, if they don't I will steal from them"

There was now a heavy silence between them.

"I cannot tell you how deeply I am indebted to you," said the deputy minister. "Thank you is too weak. Let me assure you that as of now you have in me a lifelong friend, a protector. It is as if we have jumped over a gun and vowed loyalty to one another. I shall be your loyal friend forever."

Sewyew was not taken in by these words. False friends on a long journey perform oaths of loyalty at every stream, the saying goes. He knew the man would betray him the next chance he got though he will have to repay the debt too. That was Sewyew's calculation, what he would have done if he were in the deputy's place. Sewyew had planned to get the deputy minister on his side, to lull and disarm his vigilance and then to strike. Sewyew was not ready to forget the beating and humiliations and he could never pardon the deputy minister for putting him in a situation where he had to be separated from his dark eyeglasses. The one who wounds may forget but the wounded never does.

Sewyew asked right there and then to be assigned as head of the important North America desk. He did get the post but weeks later when he went at night to sleep with a cheap whore he found out that Jegnaw had died completely. With the woman's mocking laugher ringing in his ears, he had gone back to his own cold bed to sob till dawn. In the morning he went to work as if nothing had ever changed. Too cowardly to go ahead with the suicide he had briefly contemplated, he vowed to live on making the lives of others miserable in all possible ways. He had to take revenge on the deputy minister too. A mission of hate, a vendetta—this was what gave existence purpose and really defined life. Well, at least in the city and the country he called home.

The Woman With A Grievance

She woke up drenched in sweat. Her husband slept on, snoring like an old Fiat truck overloaded with sacks of coffee groaning its way up a steep mountain road. There was a smile on her face, she felt elated.

"I have to kill him," she said to herself. The realization that she did hate her husband and wanted to kill him filled her with joy. It was as if a big load had been taken off her tired shoulders. With a sardonic smile she looked at her snoring husband. You are going to die, she whispered to him. Die! Die! Die!

There was nothing out of the ordinary in her wanting to kill her husband, she knew. Any other woman who had to bear the pain and humiliation I had to endure would do the same was her conclusion. And she was sure no one would condemn her for being happy with the realization that she had to kill to wash off her shame. She was one of the multitudes who are uncomfortable with their hate and relieved only when they stop denying acknowledgment and expression to their base and condemnable passions. Admit your sin and fear no devil as people say.

She got out of bed, finished her washing fast and left their ram-shackled house to walk up to the villa of the tenquai, witch doctor, near the Menelik Palace. Sorcery was a business that paid as handsomely as selling coffins in the death filled City but she had never bothered to wonder why many tenquais live near palaces and wealthy residential districts. The earlier she went the better, she knew. What with the tenquai now used to drinking whisky and getting tipsy by late afternoon, you never knew if he conjured the proper devil or some charlatan with horns and a tail who has no real powers but demanded the sky for nothing.

She knocked at the door. A huge man with protruding eyes opened the door.

"The Master is asleep," he said in a voice that sounded as if it had traveled long distance from his belly.

"This is a matter of life and death," she said firmly, pushing and trying to get in.

He could have stopped her but he chose to let her in saying "Isn't it always."

She found herself in the room she knew which was covered by rugs made of white and black sheep- skin. She sank into a red sofa. The living room smelt of incense and perfume. Sorcery does pay, she said to herself.

After ten minutes, the tenquai came in. The man who had been her witch doctor for far too many years she cared to remember was small and wiry. He had brown mocking eyes, was totally bald and had a full and slightly pouting mouth many women had found sensuous. She rose to greet him.

"Aha, Weizero Tenfu, sit down, sit down", said the tenquai with a smile that made him look sympathetic. He came over and they exchanged the customary four kisses on the cheeks.

"Sit down," said the witch doctor again. 'What brings you so early in the morning? You know the spirits we wake up early are too demanding."

"I will not be asking their services for now," she informed him. "I want your help only."

"But I am their instrument," said the tenquai. "My life has been theirs since I was a child, what I do is their act, what I do they always know. Do you want tea or coffee?"

She declined. "I am sure they would understand me," she said. "You give your life to someone for decades and what do you get in return? Punishment. Condemnation to die!"

"Come, come my sister," said the tenquai soothingly. "Nothing can be as bad as that. Why don't you tell me what is the problem?"

"Nothing can be as bad, you say? Is condemning you to death child's play? Is this what I deserve after all the loyalty I gave."

"I suspect you are angry at your husband," said the tenquai.

"I don't know why I bother to tell you seeing you know it without my saying so," said the woman in honest admiration. "I am more than angry at him. I want to kill him."

"I am not surprised," said the witch doctor. "At least he is someone you know very well. I have to deal with people who kill without any discernible motive or reason and think it is sublime and not pedestrian like killing for a cause."

"I lived with him for more than thirty five years," the woman said. "But do I know him? Not at all. The face I saw everyday was not his real face."

"Even our back is a stranger to us," the tenquai said knowing full well that many people live and die without ever showing their true face. "What did he do?"

But the woman was not to be rushed.

"Six children I bore for him. He married me when I still smelled of my mother's milk. Child- birth wasted me, took away my beauty, ravaged my body, but did I complain? Never. He chased other women but I never looked at another man in that way. Of the six children I bore, you know only three survived, one died of a sickness, two were taken by the Red Terror, the remaining three fled to the Sudan and then went to the USA. Two have done well there while one has turned into a drunkard. Isn't the womb of a mother of various shades and colors? The two regularly send us money and God is to be blessed we have not lacked many things. We are in our late sixties and tell me is this time to jump from one bed into another like a cursed rabbit?"

"Did he?"

"Of course he must have done. Otherwise, where could I get the cursed disease?"

The tenquai took his time to look at her. He knew she was a simple and uncomplicated woman and that, such women, when aggrieved and out for vengeance, could be ruthless and dangerous.

"What disease?" he asked.

"What disease but the most terrible one. The modern scourge!"

"AIDS?"

"Yes, AIDS," she confirmed.

"How did you know?"

"How do I know? Doesn't the hyena know the donkey's meat? The doctor told me," she said with a trace of impatience in her voice.

"What doctor?"

'The doctor, that is who. The one who examines you before you could go to America."

"Were you going there?"

"Yes, both of us. Our sons had called us. You know everyone who is anyone is going to America. Even that slut neighbor of mine was there and since she came back wearing American clothes and shoes she has been giving us hell. Invite her to coffee and she will complain that she left real coffee in Washington. As if we are not the source of coffee for the whole world! Anyway, our sons called us over to get what they call a Green Card, to resettle there and be with them."

"They do not want to come back here?"

"To what? To misery and suffering? Only pigs like to roll in the mud. Ato Lemma told me that even many wild animals have fled either to Kenya or the Sudan. What do you say to that? People more learned than ignorant me say you cannot avoid death or going to America. Who are we to say different? Over there you live good, you have cars, nice houses, good food, plenty of money. That's what they say and that is why even old people like us go through the humiliation and loss of face to get there. We are not getting any younger, it is thanks to the Almighty that we survived up to now though I wonder sometimes if He is not punishing us by letting us live under such conditions. If our children are not coming back, we agreed we have to go there and pass some years with them. So, the doctor comes in."

"They do not give you visa or permission to resettle unless you go to the doctor?"

"If that was the only humiliation. You have to line up for hours outside the visa office. They ask you personal questions and they act arrogantly and do everything to humiliate you. The day you get the visa you have lost all the face that your parents and ancestors had given you. Humiliation, I tell you. The whites are like the clay pot that has fallen on good times and is breaking the stone. You go to the doctor and get examined all over. You give them your blood and they tell you if you have any disease like the curse I mentioned earlier."

The tenquai knew of the humiliation. Many clients had come begging him to help them win the so- called DV lottery that will assure them entry into the USA. He did not know what the DV stood for but he had realized that it symbolized, in its own limited way, the loss of pride and self- respect on the part of Ethiopians. A proud people and country have been forced to bear humiliation and shame. Young and old, every one was abandoning the country to go to America and there, somebody had told him, most just drive taxis or serve as waiters in bars or do menial jobs they would never do in their own country.

"A person exiled from his country is like a broken horse

whom everyone can saddle and ride," said the tenquai softly. "'Sew bageru' as we say. You are somebody only in your own country where your first tears have wetted the soil. These days you know we are not even sure we have a country. Did they tell you themselves you have the cursed thing?"

"Tell me, you ask? Does the donkey bray softly?"

The tenquai noticed that the woman could possibly turn hysterical.

"The doctor didn't tell me to my face that I had it but they rejected my visa application, "said the woman

"They do that only if you have the disease?"

"That is what Weizero Bogaletch said. She knows the visa process very well since she has been traveling to and fro so often."

"It could be some problem with your answers to their questions," the tenquai stated. "I have heard they ask a lot of questions to trap you in a lie."

"As if a lie is not white and it is not the ferenji who invented every lie on earth!" she scoffed. "How would you explain then the welts which had appeared on my arms?"

"What welts?"

"Tow months ago there were big welts on my arms and then they disappeared. They say it is a sign of AIDS."

"Who says?"

"Weizero Meaza whose son had died from the disease. He had welts exactly like mine before he died she says."

"Did the doctor see the welts?"

"No. They had disappeared by the time I went for the examination."

"You know even doctors make mistakes about such things let alone a woman like Meaza who has no training. Infections causing welts and skin marks are aplenty in our City."

The woman did not look convinced.

"You did have sexual relations with your husband?" the tenquai asked.

"Six months or so ago he came one night drunk and groped for me. There is no rest for women and we have not taken the communion much as I had been wanting to." Older couples take communion together and with it they vow celibacy.

"Did your husband have the welts?"

"How would I know? He could have had welts the size of the Entoto. Since he has gone on pension he hardly stays home and I rarely see him, dressed or otherwise."

"Why are you angry at him really?"

She sighed. He waited for her to speak but she took her time. The tenquai looked down at his black and expensive loafers.

"I hate him," she said finally. "I want him dead."

"I understood as much," said the tenquai. "But why?" He had always asked why though most of his clients have been surprised by his assumption that murder needs a motive. He knew most Ethiopians who publicly express a desire to kill would not do the act while the real killers usually wear a smile on their faces and profess love to their neighbors and enemies.

"For all the suffering I had to endure," she replied. "He owes me my youth, a life actually. I had to bear all the pain while he drunk and whored all his life. I am sure he must have given me the disease."

"You have come many times to me but you never told me you had such pain," said the tenquai. "I could have helped. You could have divorced too."

"How could I with all my children? Give them over to a step- mother who would starve and beat them to death? It was something I could never do; better I suffer to save them from seeing the scorching face of a step- mother. By the time the children left, it was too late really. What do we expect of marriage anyway if not some joy and plenty of pain?"

The unmarried witch doctor did not venture an opinion.

"You are sold off by your parents long before you reach puberty," went on the woman, "handed over to a man you had never seen. He could be as ugly as a monkey's behind aside from being a brute like most men. He could stink like an outhouse; he could have some undeclared skin disease, no matter. Arranged marriage, the deal is made before you stop suckling at your mother's breast. Is this fair, I ask you? They cut off your nails so that you cannot scratch at your husband on the wedding night. They expect you to fight though since no fight means you are an easy woman. Come wedding night, your half drunk husband throws himself at you with as much sensitivity as a rushing flood. He enjoys your scream, the whole family enjoys your cry of pain and the blood smeared cloth or bed- sheet is shown to all and accepted with ululation. Welcome to the world. What a welcome. By thirteen you feel torn, soiled, abused and old. Is it a surprise if I hate him?"

"Much as I sympathize," said the tenquai cautiously, "you cannot hold your husband responsible for the ills of the whole society. Customs change with time. Here in the City nowadays, they do not get married before they have slept together. What do you say to that? There is also the young girl who shot dead the man who abducted her by force."

"Good for them who do not get forced into marriage without knowing what awaits them", said the woman "At least they know what they are getting into or what is going to get into them."

She could not hold back her laughter and the tenquai joined her with a roaring laugh. When they subsided, the tenquai said: "I think you are bored," he told the woman. "A whole day eaten away by doing nothing can be so tiring."

"Why do you say doing nothing?" she protested. "I still cook, clean the house, wash the clothes, go to the market to buy food. I work. A woman's work never ends and is never appreciated."

"But you are not satisfied," persisted the tenquai. "You feel cheated out of a life, as you said, while you think he had and is still having a good time. You blame him. I am sure you do not hate him deep down. Like most women of your kind, married at an early age to men they did not know or love, you had long ago learnt just to tolerate the man, to see through him, to ignore him even. Mind you there are many arranged marriages that turn out good. My parent's case is an example. But not all are examples of harmony. You have solid grievances, some justifiably against your husband, but most against the society. There is little you can do, little I can do. If you want I can call the spirits and ask them but I know what they will say."

"But I have…"

He interrupted her. "I know you want to do something but do not rush to take any drastic action. I am sure he spends most of his time with pensioners like himself in some bar or 'tej bet'. The problem is that you do not talk amongst yourselves, maybe you never were and you are no longer friends. Let me tell you what I will do. I will arrange with the spirits and we will make your husband stay home with you. Or take you to visit the monasteries, your relatives in the countryside. In the meantime, you check on the real reason for the rejection of the visa application and you reapply if you really feel you should go. I have heard the embassy people themselves also sell the visa at a price if you have to go at all costs. I for one think that for good or worse our own country is good enough for all of us."

"You will talk to the spirits?" she asked expectantly.

"Sure," he promised. "This time in the morning it is Shadiya I would probably get but it is ok. She is moody and capricious but she likes to help women. Wait one moment", said the tenquai and left the room.

The tenquai called the huge man who served as his assistant and also as a servant and ordered him to go the woman's house immediately and to summon her husband. When the aide left, the tenquai rejoined the woman. She got up in respect.

"Sit down," he told her as he sat down himself. "Here is a packet of special incense you are going to burn every evening," he said giving her a packet he fished out of his coat pocket. "It will soothe and please the spirits."

The woman thanked him profusely and wanted to pay but he declined this one time, and told her she will pay him later on, much later on. The woman left the compound relieved much like people who unload their nightmares and anxieties on others and feel better even if they have found no solution for their predicaments.

The husband came accompanied by the tenquai's assistant and he was ushered into the same room in which his wife had been sitting just a while ago.

"Good of you to come at such a short notice,' said the tenquai.

"Who can dare to ignore the summons coming from you?" said the old man with a smile. The tenquai noted that the man looked much older than the wife.

"I dared to call you over to share some information with you,' said the tenquai."

"Shall I serve you tea or coffee?"

The man having declined the offer, the tenquai continued, "As I said, some information has reached me. You know I get a lot of confidential information. It is between the man or woman, the spirits and poor me. These walls of mine have no ears whatsoever, the spirits have seen to that a long time ago. Secrets die with me. Yet, from time to time, with the permission of the spirits, I have divulged some information to save people, to avoid catastrophes."

The tenquai saw he had the old man's complete attention.

"I have come across an information that could be of interest to you," went on the tenquai. "To you and your wife that is. How many years since I knew her, your wife? More than I care to remember lest I feel old. "He smiled. "You know Ato Kiros Abraham?"

"Who doesn't? He is the richest man in our district."

"The same," said the tenquai. "A widower for long. Almost your age I would say. He is a man with much money and powerful connections. Some say his mother hailed from the northern region, you know from where our present rulers come. It is a useful ethnic background to have these days. I hear he is, I don't know how to put it, he is attracted by your wife."

"Attracted?" The surprise was evident in the voice of the old man.

"Yes, attracted," said the witch doctor. "Your wife, as you

surely know, is still a very attractive woman. Ato Kiros, it is said, is actually wildly in love."

"At his age? With my wife?"

"The folly of love strikes hard and unexpected, specially as you get older. Mind you, he has total respect for your honor and has not up to now intended to express his feelings in public or to your wife. But the thing is there. He has a lot of wealth and he is, from what I hear, still skilful at courting. Not that all this will matter since you and your wife are in harmony and happy."

The old man bit his lip, deep in thought. What figures is he seeing in the clouds within his head, the tenquai wondered.

"You know I deal with spirits and the Devil," said the tenquai stating the obvious. "I am trying to say I know the road traveled by evil, the way a small dark seed slowly grows into an ominous and devastating problem. Steps must be taken to nip the possibility in the bud."

"He cannot dare approach my wife. I will kill him."

"As you must," agreed the tenquai with tact. "I don't expect any less from you. As we used to say, one's wife and country are untouchable by others, by foreigners. Yet, it is better to take preventive steps. I am sure your wife, who does not know of Ato Kiros' intentions, would reject him if he were to approach her as you are happily married."

The old man again remained silent.

"Yes, prevention is advisable," went on the tenquai. "Remove temptations from the path of men lest they succumb to their weakness. Isn't the organ of the donkey inside his stomach? No need to brandish, to provoke."

"What do you advise?" the old man asked.

"Stay with her, spend time with her in your house. I suggest also you take your wife to Zuquala, Debre Libanos, Yoftah Giorgis in Quara, to Waldiba even. Praying in these holy monasteries will do you both good. Later on you can even go to visit your sons in America. What do you say?"

I will do as you say was what the old man said. He did not say he loved his wife but the tenquai was not expecting any such declaration. Even where love existed he knew few males of his generation would openly admit to being in love and thus, in their view, weak. A wife was like land, valuable property to be protected and to be disposed of only by the owner. A lost wife did not primarily mean derailed love but mainly a lost, shattered face. In some areas of rural Ethiopia, if a woman is divorced by her husband he can remarry while she can do so too only by leaving the village since it is considered an affront to this manliness (wendinet) if she were to marry in the same village no matter if he had taken another wife already. Most men easily said I cherish my land, my property but find it ever hard to express such a sentiment about their spouses. The defunct military regime had disturbed the order of things by nationalizing all land and turning all the men into undeclared serfs with reduced power even in their own household. But a wife was still a wife. The old man could very well vow to kill the wealthy man if the latter dared to proposition his wife but deep down he knew the wealthy end up by having their way. Especially rich men with even a dose of the right ethnic blood were becoming mini kings everywhere. It was wise to listen to the tenquai. After all, what choice do I have, the old man asked himself. Who dares disobey a witch doctor with the Devil on his side?

The Garbage Baby

*T*he policeman's boot landed a vicious kick on her skinny butt. She yelped and uttered a foul curse. He kicked her again and before she could rise he had fallen on his knees and pinned her down. His breath smelt of the cheap Araqie that was sold in the slums of the city, his teeth were green, yellow and black, rotten by too much coffee, Kat and cheap cigarettes. His head moved ominously down as he tried to kiss her. She bit his lips and drew blood and he screamed.

She woke up, her heart beating wildly, her body damp with perspiration. It was always at this point that she woke up. Not after relishing the sight of him writhing in pain and screaming again and again in agony but just as she bit him and he utters only one miserly scream. It was a dream she had almost every night. The policeman did exist in her life, he was in his thirties, did not smoke, did drink araqie and whatever cheap alcohol he got his hands on and he had been after her for the whole of last year. Dodging him had not been easy, what with him being a policeman with power (and the stick and the pistol) and she a mere street girl with tattered clothes and an often- empty stomach. She was fifteen years old and with the starved and skinny body of a girl much younger than that.

Some called her "Famine Child", others had named her "Garbage Baby". Her mother brought her over to the City during the time of the Great Famine (no, not of last year or that of 1973 but in 1984). Thousands of the famished descended on the City just as the military rulers had imported enough whisky for their great bash to honor the founding of the Vanguard Party. The cruel dictator was anxiously awaiting the momentous day of the party's founding congress, where he would be crowned a demi-God by his own puppets, and he was in no mood to allow the starved and dying thousands, who wore the real face of the tortured country, to enter the City. Armed soldiers and special police ringed the City and closed the entry points leaving the starving, who had trekked for weeks and seen their relatives and kin die on the long route, the choice of facing death by bullets or death by slow starvation. Despite the closure, however, many managed to enter the City and to increase the already swollen number of beggars. The dictator had his day enjoying the usual praise heaped upon him by his programmed and fawning flunkies. The news of his brutality towards his own suffering people and his callousness exhibited by the millions of Birr spent for the Congress while millions of people starved was, unfortunately for him, to be headline news all over the world.

Her mother did make it to the City. The old father and three children had already starved to death and the daughter was the only one left for the mother. People in the City were poor (weren't they always?) but kind-hearted. The little they had they shared with the starving who were after all their own country folk. The mother lasted for only a few months. One morning, she just did not wake up. The exhausted body and spirit gave up. The three- year old girl was crying her heart out when someone observed that the mother was immobile and approached to investigate. The mother and child were sleeping on a pile of garbage, more specifically on a torn and tattered mattress stained with urine and God knows what and thrown on the garbage heap. A municipal truck came much later to take the corpse away. There was no hurry, the City had more than its share of uncollected corpses on the street every day and just a few years back the government itself was exposing the mutilated corpses of its opponents on the streets for all too see and tremble. A boy slightly older than her, she was to learn later he was actually six at the time, had approached her before the municipal truck had even arrived and taken her away, away from her mother's corpse, away to a life on the streets. She had often wondered what would have happened to her if the municipal truck had picked her up instead or the police taken her to the station. Not much would have changed she had concluded later after coming to know of the fate of other street children. She had followed the boy, taken the hand he had offered. He had appeared to her as a savior, one of her lost brothers and he had looked so sure of himself.

He was a veteran of the streets, born of a beggar woman and a soldier who had raped her and beaten her senseless before leaving her for dead near the St. George Church. His mother had drunk herself to death when he was just three and he had continued to beg, to sleep on the street, outside church compounds, to beg, to avoid the hated police and to survive. Six years old and he thought he already knew much of what was to know of the street life. He had seen the little girl crying in confusion and fear next to the dead body of her mother and his heart went out to her. He had already seen too many dead bodies on the streets, beggars who do not wake up, young people shot by the soldiers and the security police, victims of murderous thugs. He hung out with a gang of street boys, many older than himself, they looked after one another, the older boys had more privileges (you have to search the sniffing petrol or glue for them for example) but they took care of the young. They shared what they gained working as coolies, pick pocketing when they could, begging, hustling and coning at the bus stations where the rural people alighted from the buses confused and frightened (and made vulnerable) by the City full of cars and so many people and big buildings and fenced houses. When the little emaciated girl with the round and beautiful eyes followed him, the young boy vowed to himself that he would defend her for all his life. He told her his name was Getaneh and she had told him hers: Tsigereda (Rose). Her dead father had given her the name-- she was his favorite. Getaneh laughed good- naturedly at her rural accent. The gang was made up of four boys other than Getaneh. None of them were older than ten. The oldest, Shenkute, was the undisputed head.

"Why did you bring her?" Shenkute asked Getaneh when he arrived with her at their usual lounging place near the Piazza. He talked clipping and biting into his words, a style deliberately chosen by him to sound tough like the veteran street boys who talked as if they had to pay tax for any long sentence they uttered.

Getaneh left her alone, and the gang huddled together to talk in whispers.

"Her mother died on her," Getaneh explained.

"So?" Shenkute sounded unimpressed. "How many children are abandoned by their mothers? She could even be lucky if her mother was anyone like The Fesam's mother."

The boy referred to as the fesam/farter smiled. He got his nickname because he could fart on command and can always foul any surrounding. He was eight and like all the rest his hair was almost shaved with only a small patch left in front (it was called the kuncho or temari kurt, student cut). His mother, who did love him, had tried to kill him three times before the police, who considered her crazy, put her in the Amanuel mental institution where they gave her the routine treatment- hands and feet tied, electric shocks, brutal treatment- and managed to really drive her crazy and towards suicide. Yet another unlamented victim in a City full of crushed souls. The Farter had fond memories of his mother and did not share Shenkute's opinion though he did not contradict him.

Shenkute broke the circle and approached her.

"What's your name?"

When she told him he laughed. "What an accent. She's a "finchit" too," he said noticing the small attractive gap between two of her front teeth. She smiled and he added, "a dimple too. No wonder Getaneh could not resist."

The boys all laughed and she, uncomfortable, looked at Getaneh who came over and stood next to her. She sought and clutched his hand.

Shenkute spoke again: "I am Shenkute. You already know Getaneh. The fesam over there is Kifle. Do not sleep near him because he could poison you. That other one with the scar on his cheek is Abebe whose real name is actually Addis Abeba. Finally, the timid looking one is Solomon. He is as timid as mad man Tadesse who roams around naked in the Piazza."

She smiled.

"Yes, smile," said Shenkute. "You can go places with that dimple. No sniffing for you and no smoking. You stay with Getaneh and do as he tells you. Got it?"

She did not really understand him but that she was to stay with Getaneh pleased her. All of a sudden she remembered her mother and burst into tears calling for her mother. It took them all ten minutes to soothe her and make her stop crying. The Farter was also in tears remembering his own mother.

Getaneh took her along wherever he went, fed her most of the time more than he ate himself. His group accepted her, she started to beg, to get acquainted with the City and its streets. Most of the time, they slept near a church compound depending in which part of the City they found themselves in but care had to be taken not to cross other street groups who had a strong notion of territory and its protection. Getaneh did not sniff petrol and she did not choose to follow the others who did so, arambists as they were called, even when she was hungry and sniffing petrol or glue would have helped her to bear the ache. She had seen their glazed eyes, observed what the petrol did to them and concluded that this was not for her at all. Shenkute smoked foul smelling cigarette butts they collected from the street for him. Later on, she saw most street children chewing on kat but she never took up the habit of chewing the mildly hallucinogenic green leaves.

Within a few years, the streets were home to more and more people. Older City folks who had fallen on hard times, young and old from the rural areas fleeing from war and hunger, amputated ex soldiers, victims of unacknowledged famines, women and men, young and old, all fell down to the street, homeless as they were called, "menged- adari (the ones who sleep on the street) and not any more "Berendah- adari" since there were no more verandahs being built or accepting uninvited sleepers. The competition became intense, the more people became poorer, the less the relatively fortunate ones became generous. It was as if most of the City people were in the same hole, some with a shelter, however dilapidated, they called home and others without just like her.

When she was ten, the military government collapsed. In the confusion of the last days, Getaneh and his friends were able to lay their hands on abandoned automatic guns that they hoped to sell for considerable sums. Hiding the guns was not difficult, the new conquerors were harsh and menacing but like a monk in a brothel they were out of place, alien to the City that did not welcome them in the first place.

And for the first time she learnt that they were not all Ethiopians but members of ethnic groups. She did not know to what group she belonged and did not care. Kifle the Farter was however found out to be a member of the northern ethnic group whose sons had come to power and it was not long before he was approached by the cadres and asked to be an informer.

"They want me to be a dirty joro tebi," he told them using the pejorative word (ear sucker) for informer. "How could I? I do not even speak their language?"

"How did they know you came from their region?" asked Shenkute.

"How would I know," said Kifle. "Maybe my father's name. Did you know it is Gidey?" They shook their head in a no. "The stupid policeman Haielom who is now working for them knows it. He may have told them."

They huddled and discussed the whole development. In the end, they agreed to allow him to be an informer, get his pay (which he would share with them) and inform on nobody to cause any harm. The Farter was now fifteen, Shenkute almost eighteen, and Getaneh thirteen. Street life became difficult because it was too crowded. By far too many people were sleeping on the street, thousands were begging, homeless children were in their many thousands. And the new police were crude and brutal, they treated City-folk like conquered people, uneducated and ignorant they hated and feared all City dwellers and tried to make their lives miserable.

The Terror of a policeman, the very one who was to make her life miserable, saw her when she turned thirteen. She wore baggy clothes but tattered as they were they did not really hide her budding breasts and shapely legs. She was selling Lubar, one of the independent newspapers, when he accosted her. The government was claiming to be tolerant of the free press while cracking on the sale of the same newspapers, which made her and others like her victims. She was just coming out of the Bambolina Bar when he grabbed at her viciously.

"Don't you know better than to sell this trash?" he barked at her, grabbing with his other hand the newspapers she was carrying.

He was tall and thin, with a bulging Adam's apple that made him look ugly. She looked into his blood shot eyes.

"You want me to beg or to steal," she retorted boldly.

The kick was vicious and landed on her butt with a thud. She yelped. He dragged her along as he insulted her, her mother, her father and all her kin.

"I will take you to the station and you will find out how we deal with smart mouths," he threatened. Passers by looked at her but none intervened—time had passed since people with courage had disappeared.

By the time they reached the side road which served as a shortcut to the police station he dragged her to the side of the path, away from the sight of passer bys and said to her: "You are a pretty girl underneath all this dirt. I will spare you for now. No prison for you now and you will get back your newspaper." He gave her back her papers and went on: "you cannot sell this or any other such trash in public places and bars. There is a law against it. If I catch you next time, I will be harsh. I am nice to you and you will have to be nice to me."

She had lived long on the streets to know what he was hinting at. She looked at him with impassive eyes and with a defiance he mistook for fear. From that day on, the policeman tried to trap her and since his beat seemed to be in and around the places she and Getaneh frequented it was not long before he found them selling newspapers and whisked them off to the police station. They were beaten up, lectured at length and released. They looked out for the policeman and avoided him but two months later a round up of street children was made one night and all of them were netted by the police as they slept huddled together for warmth. They were all taken outside the City and abandoned in the hyena- infested forests. Getaneh, who managed to take her out of the forest and into a village nearby from where they made their way back to the City the next afternoon, saved her from the sad fate of those eaten by hyenas.

Their group broke up eventually. His employers sent Kifle to Dire Dawa. Shenkute joined the army when the war broke out between the government and its former northernmost allies. Solomon moved to another area in the City while Abebe left them all to join those he called liberation guerrillas. It was she and Getaneh who stayed on and she had no complaints since she loved him as a brother and enjoyed his protection. But her world was to be shattered by the cruel policeman who, after watching her often with Getaneh, decided to remove the person conceived by him as the "competition". Getaneh was arrested by the policeman, falsely accused of stealing and jailed. Once in jail people are often forgotten and Getaneh joined hundreds others who were languishing in crowded jails without ever being brought before a court of law. With Getaneh out of the way, it was easier for the policeman to keep an eye on her. One evening he followed her to her secluded sleeping place under a wooden bridge in the Yeka area and raped her.

No one heard her scream or if they had none came to her rescue. He slapped her into silence and raped her. When he had had his way he slapped her again ("talk about this and you shall die!") and left. She sobbed the whole night, curled unto herself, feeling bruised, wounded and dirty. Used to the smell of her own unwashed body she now could not stand the smell he had imprinted on her body and nose. In the morning, despite feeling sore she went to the nearby stream and washed herself again and again. She knew there was nothing she could do against the policeman. He was from the "chosen" ethnic group, a policeman, and thus above the law. It was the word of a street girl against that of a policeman and she was old enough to know her words would weigh no more than the feather of a baby pigeon and that she would actually land in more trouble. Getaneh was not there to help her take revenge and God only knew when they would release him, if ever. Frustrated and in tears she was but she did not ignore the fire in her guts calling for vengeance.

She felt as if she had aged many years overnight. She kept no company though there were other street boys and girls who wanted to befriend her. Listless and emaciated she moved into another district in order to avoid the policeman. One early morning, hungry and desperate, she had gone to the huge garbage dump in Aware to rummage for leftover food when she found the abandoned half naked baby crying its heart out. She could see it was a baby boy and there was no one in the vicinity. She did not hesitate one minute before picking the baby up into her arms and walking away from the garbage dump.

"My own little garbage baby," she cooed unto his ears. The baby had stopped crying and was now looking at her with round and innocent eyes. "I will find you milk soon," she promised the baby as tears streaked down her cheeks. A smile lit her face, her tooth-gap and dimples visible. "You will grow up and avenge me," she told the baby. "What if I call you Getaneh?"

She thought the baby smiled in agreement.

The Mob

It spilled down the narrow street like a vigorous flood with destruction as its mission. It was made up of hundreds but surged like one, bonded by a frothing hate stemming out of many separate frustrations. The street trembled under its feet, some shod, many others bare, all advancing.

"Do not let him escape," one shouted and the others boomed a Never that rolled down the street and reached the running man who was catapulted into more speed by the fire of the words. As It run after the victim, each and every one of its members felt alive, for once they had a purpose, for once they were not the helpless victims waiting for the sword to fall. Every one felt powerful, in possession of his manhood (It hardly ever had no female members), the judge and executioner. All flexed their tiny muscles with pride and suddenly- found power, humiliation and hunger forgotten, frustrations ignored, determined to do unto him the victim what the powerful had been doing unto them for long.

It turned to a smaller street and the ones in front came face to face with two policemen armed with Kalashnikov rifles. Hesitantly the mob slowed down in the face of real power.

"Is It a Mob?" one of the policemen asked.

The crowd answered with a deafening yes.

"Smelling blood? Chasing a victim?" the other policeman queried.

The yes was thunderous.

"Proceed then," said the policemen. And It surged onwards, promising havoc.

It could not be stopped. It knew no law, no restraints. From Pretoria to Nairobi, from Kampala and Kigali to Freetown, It ruled the streets from time to time, emerging sporadically and with force, gathering all the hate and vile on its way, rising to a crescendo with the foul cries for blood, united in the search for the destruction of a life, simmering and seething till It found gratification in the pain and death of another human being.

"Do you see him?" one asked.

"There he is," said one pointing a bony finger at the distance. Every one raised a hand to point a finger at the distance. It was a gesture that came easily to them after years of repressive rule and the carnage called the Red Terror during which they were forced to denounce not only others but themselves too.

It was catching up with its victim who was tiring it seemed. It had also swollen in size.

"What did he do?" one asked as he fell in step and joined the others.

No one answered.

"Is he a thief?"

No answer.

"A rapist?"

None replied but all continued to advance. The heat was intense and It was raising dust as It run after the victim. The smell of unwashed bodies joined the rising dust to assail the noses but none noticed it.

"There must be a reason," the same man shouted. "There is no mob without a reason."

"What do you mean?" another bespectacled and intellectual-looking man protested as he overtook others and came close to the one who had been talking. "A mob is a mob precisely because it has no reason. Only an end."

"Nonsense", the other shot back as he panted and tried to keep his place. "The Interhamwe hated the Tutsis, the Baggaras detest the Dinkas, the Somalis hate us all. What will similar mobs in other parts of Africa say of us if we have no reason for chasing the man."

"He is uncircumcised," said one other man. The Mob uttered a collective cry of "shame!" expressing its hatred for the uncut.

"I think he also stole," ventured another one.

"Death to the leba! Death to thieves!" shouted many as the mob closed the distance between it and the hapless victim who was now gasping for breath and about to collapse.

About the same time in other cities and towns almost all over Africa other Mobs with murder in their hearts were catching up on their quarries.

"Burn him," shouted one.

"At the current prices of kerosene and petrol, no way," said another.

"Implosion," another insisted copying the South African method of dousing the victim with petrol and making him also drink a mouthful before setting him afire.

"Torch him," proposed a sickly man who showed no sign of being tired from the running.

"At the current price of petrol and kerosene?" the man who had protested earlier shouted again.

It was catching up with the victim and sensing a kill the Mob quivered in anticipation. Kill! The din rose up to the clouds, up and above the dust, high up to the sky but as usual there was no reaction from He who is supposed to dwell up there.

The victim collapsed to the ground, exhausted and hopeless.

The Mob encircled him. Brutal kicks landed on the man on

the ground. "Leba!", "Rapist!", "Weshela", the Mob shrieked.

"He is from the North," cried, nay screamed, one and the Mob fell back.

"Turn him over," ordered one and a man with a hunchback turned the beaten man over on his back.

"He has the sign on his temples," shouted many.

"He is from the North," cried others in fear.

"The Mob finishes what it has begun," said one from within the crowd.

"Yes!" shouted a few.

"No!" warned many others afraid of the government wrath.

The Mob was shouting yes and no back and forth when an armed and obviously drunk soldier pushed people aside and approached the fallen man.

"Mob justice, is it?" he asked cocking his rifle.

"A bloody thief for sure," he said as he emptied his bullets into the body of the fallen man.

The Mob dispersed in silence, deflated like a balloon that has lost its air. It felt betrayed, denied its own orgy of violence and blood- letting.

"We don't even have the right to be a Mob," complained one. "Africa must be ashamed of us."

The next day the government controlled newspaper reported as first page news the sad death of Demissie Biru who was "killed by a Mob of vagabonds who mistook him for a thief" as he was running to practice for the upcoming all - country athletic competition.

The Rumors Bar

*I*f you have ever been to Uganda you would have seen the Rumors Restaurant on your way from Entebbe Airport to downtown Kampala. The owner of the Rumors Bar in the City I have been writing about has never been to Uganda and would be angered if you were to tell her she had copied the name of her bar from one enterprising Ugandan bar owner. The Rumors Bar was formerly The Bar of No Surprises and before that it had some other names dictated by the political wind that prevailed. In the Rumors Bar, tall tales get told as tongues wax lyrical after a good helping of the potent Dagim araqie and the house specialty, a cocktail drink called Damtew/ Bulldozer made up of some whisky, vodka and of God knows what else.

Matteos was as regular to the bar as the flies around the tables. His table companions almost every night were his longtime friends, Misikir and Tamrat.

"I could tell you the story of the hapless man who proposed to the younger sister and was married to the elder one instead," Matteos promised his friends as they met one cold Tuesday evening in the Rumors Bar.

Procedure demanded that they should ask "Rumor or True?" and they did so.

"More true than the eight o'clock news", said Matteos safely. Any declaration had the chance of being more truthful than the news over the State controlled media.

"The young man saw this Harari girl who was strikingly beautiful. He followed her to her house to get her address and then convinced his family to ask for her hand. Which they did." Matteos smiled and took a sip from his Bulldozer. "Little did he know that she had an older sister who was still single. The family of the girl agreed, took the dowry and the marriage night the elder sister came as the bride wearing her veil. There was no way the younger one could be married off with the elder one standing out there without a husband shunned by all like a stick that has been dipped into something foul. He, however, thought she was his chosen. At night, you know most of us go to bed with women after putting out the light and that was what he did too. This doing it in the dark only has a lot to do with our belief that the whole act is a sin but that's another story. He took her virginity after much struggle, screams and suffering for him too since Harari girls are infibulated. In the morning he woke up to find himself next to a long faced plain looking girl who was coyly calling him my husband."

"What did he do?" Tamrat asked. He was the shorter and darker member of the trio and the chain smoker par excellence.

"What could he do? She bore him two sons and one morning he decamped and came to the City."

"The heartless brute," said Miskir, the sentimental of the group. "Leaving his children."

The wife's family took them in," added Matteos trying to mollify his friend though he did not really know what had happened to the wife and the two sons. Giving sad tales false happy endings was not frowned upon in the Rumors Bar. One grasped at the stars especially on a dark winter night.

"The City is full of abandoned children," said Tamrat. "I know one who was found abandoned on a gravestone in a cemetery. She grew up with something eerie about her and people said she had supernatural powers, sort of devilish you know. Some spirit had gone into her as she lay there with the dead. She even had a black spot in the white of her right eye just like a pretty cousin of mine."

They ordered more drinks.

"I was at court today," Matteos informed the other two. "You know what case was being heard? The case of the former officials who bought the skull of an executed man for 15 Birr."

The others did not express any surprise.

"The accused and others bought the skull at a government fund raising bazaar. That was what was known as recycling the counter revolutionaries. You shoot them dead and you sell their skulls at a bazaar. No wonder we think we are the children of Ham."

"Nonsense," said Tamrat. "We are not cursed by God from birth. We make, we decide, our own fate. It is the whites who brainwash us into believing we are cursed and, by virtue of our color, inferior."

"Talking of fate," Miskir interjected, "did you know the story of the ill-fated bus? There was this woman I shall conveniently call Yetimwerk, actually the name of one of my aunts. She was so hurt and humiliated by her husband that she decided to poison him and went to the Mercato, you know exactly where, and bought cyanide powder. There was another man whom I shall call Mekuria just like the old lion of the late Emperor who also went to the Mercato not to buy poison but to keep a rendezvous with a mistress in a sleazy hotel. These two and some other people all boarded the ill-fated bus that was to travel from the Mercato all the way to the Menelik Hospital and further. Now, the story gets really interesting. The bus was at the station, motor running, waiting for the passengers to board and the chauffeur was outside talking to a friend and waiting for the bus to fill up. Let me introduce at this time the other protagonist of the story," said Miskir enjoying their attention and taking a sip from his glass. "Ato Wasihun. He was one of the millions of ordinary City dwellers who are often trampled upon by powerful boots without ever getting a fair deal. For more than 15 years he had been a chauffeur for the bus company but he had been laid off brusquely without benefits or adequate pension. Like many others, he had flipped, you know, joined the elsewhere caste as we call the insane. He didn't roam the streets naked but he talked to himself and went more and more mad with every passing day. By some coincidence he found himself at the particular bus station and seeing the apparently chauffeur less bus with its motor running and filling up with passengers he just jumped into the driver's seat closed the doors and drove off. The passengers only realized something was amiss when Wasihun did not stop at the usual bus stops, ignored their protests and speeded instead to the Central Command Bureau of the ruling party.

"What are you up to?" the armed guard barked at Wasihun. "You can't drive a bus in there."

"I am carrying counter-revolutionaries," said Wasihun calmly. "Open up and let me in before your superiors punish you."

You know how it is with soldiers and bureaucrats. All are scared of being held responsible for something they may have failed to do. The guard lifted the roadblock and Wasihun drove his frightened passengers into the dreaded compound. To make a long story short, the security officers considered it Manna from the sky and they arrested all the passengers including Wasihun who had started to insult them. Yetimwerk was found with the cyanide pill and tortured to admit she belonged to the underground movement whose members carried cyanide pills sewn into their clothes. She refused to confess and was tortured viciously for days before being sent to the Kerchiele where she stayed behind bars for ten long years during which she lost her sanity. Mekuria confessed he belonged to a "reactionary anti-peace group" and was spared further brutal torture but kept in prison for seven long years. Wasihun was beaten up and later transferred to the mental asylum where he may still be kept."

The Rumors Bar was now filling up and at every table the clients in subdued but passionate voices were recounting captivating tales. It was an exercise in keeping trace of a people's experience. Told stories circulate, they are retold, sometimes embellished but somewhere in what may sound as a wild tale some years later there remained a kernel of the truth, a trace of what had happened to people, to all of them, to the country. Memory serves to cherish the past, the sacrifices, the sufferings endured by those who had left their footprints in history and in this way a people stood united against forgetfulness, keeping watch over its heritage.

"I still say nothing compared to the story of Zewdu who paid the ultimate sacrifice to save others," said Matteos starting out to tell his tale. "You know there were many heroes during those terrible times, hard times test a people and that generation was tested by fire and found to be like gold. But Zewdu was special. He was a coolie, a porter whose calloused shoulders carried more burdens than met the eyes of people. His cross was heavy and no one knew his secret. He was like Zewdu Wolde Amanuel who died a hero's death to save many others by hanging himself in prison. This Zewdu also joined the underground movement, took part in very many heroic actions and when he was captured he did not break under torture but committed suicide and took the secrets to the grave. I know the way you die sometimes shows the life you had but Zewdu's story is interesting not for the way he died but for what he had to live with all those years since he left his rural village and came to the City to be a lowly coolie.

Zewdu and his wife to be first met at a church. For him it was love at first sight. Her head was covered by a netela but at a fateful moment, when the 'Tabot', was coming out of its sacred place to circle the church three times, he had looked at her and she had looked back at him. Beautiful and soft brown eyes that did not blink, Nubian eyes that could fire a coward's heart and turn him into a brave man. He felt his heart skip a beat and thought he detected a mocking curl on her full and inviting lips. He was lost. Mind you this was the time of arranged marriages and he was old enough to realize that she must have been already betrothed to another but he was made foolhardy by instant love and had no doubt he would win her hand. Love makes you embrace your own delusions, doesn't it?

His father, when Zewdu asked him to intervene on his behalf, was not so convinced. I know her, was what he said, Woubet is the daughter of Mariye. Mariye was a rich peasant but Zewdu's father was not poor either. Woubet is a rebel child, added Zewdu's father. Once, she burnt the hut of her would- be husband and came back to her father's home on her wedding night. At another time, she fled from her house to avoid being married off and was brought back from the monastery she had gone to after much begging by her father. What makes you think she will marry you, asked Zewdu's father, especially when she finds out you are well into your twenties and still unmarried? But Zewdu was not to be dissuaded. He was obsessed. In the end, his father and other relatives went to the girl's house with the gifts that custom dictated ("your daughter is of course worth a mountain of gold but pray accept this humble gift as a token of our appreciation") and politely asked for her hand in the name of Zewdu. As custom demands, the girl's father refused at first. More gifts were given, a bigger dowry promised, the negotiations maintained to play out the rigors of custom. In the end, the dowry was settled, Woubet's father agreed and Zewdu was elated. The wedding feast was one of the biggest ever seen in the area and the celebrations lasted for more than a week. Raw meat, roasted meat, injera and doro wet, tej, frimba, araqie, name it and all was aplenty. It was such a big wedding that more than fifteen priests were treated for "kuntan" as a result of stuffing themselves. You know the priests are given the choicest of meats and aplenty but they overeat as if every feast was to be their last meal. The sight of fifteen priests flat on their backs, stomachs swollen, groaning on the ground and the masseurs chanting "aba kuntan..antes lemin belah,antes lemin nefah, fes tefendes"

("why did you have to eat so much, why did you have to

inflate his stomach so much, let the fart go free...") trying to relieve the ache of the suffering priests was a proud moment for the parents.

It was his best man who had to drag-carry him to the bridal bed and to the expectant Woubit. Zewdu awoke the next morning with his bride sleeping naked at his side and he could remember only his best man plying him with more and more araqie much to the amusement of his bride who did not seem to mind. He couldn't recall how he got to the bed and, more importantly, what he had done, if anything at all, in it. He brushed aside his thoughts and concentrated instead on enjoying the sight of the naked body of the beautiful girl who had now apparently become his wife. She woke up as he was staring at her shapely body.

She smiled coyly at him but did not try to cover up her body.

"I am sorry I overslept," she said in a timid voice. "You tired me last night."

"I am afraid I drank too much."

She smiled and from the floor on her side she picked a white sheet smeared red with blood. "Not that much that you could not make a woman out of me," she told him with a proud tone and he beamed back at her with satisfaction. He really felt proud and happy. The blood sheet was later exhibited to the families and the wedding guests, ululations reverberated, shots were fired and more tej and filtered tella drank and raw meat consumed with the fiery red pepper and bile dipping.

A son came first. A daughter followed. Their farm was adequate, they had many cattle and they did seem to love one another. He felt guilty for feeling so happy and went to church more often than before to praise God as he said but actually to placate the capricious deity who, he thought, did not seem to like seeing people happy. He regularly went to the faraway cattle market twice a month and stayed there for three days or so and he did good business. His mother and his best man kept his wife company while he was away on such business.

Change had to come and it came suddenly. As people say, misery is a brother and happiness just a passerby. She started becoming irritable, annoyed at him at the slightest excuse, daring to refuse his advances in bed claiming she had her monthlies, was tired, sick and whatnot. Another rural husband would have slapped her outright and had his way with her but Zewdu was a gentle, and therefore rare, man who truly loved his wife and had never raised his hand against her.

The atmosphere in the house became morose, heavy, and sad enough for the walls to shed tears and for some of the bed bugs to move elsewhere. They ate in silence if at all she agreed to eat with him. They slept in the same bed but she did not allow him to touch her, they hardly ever talked. He confided to his best man who advised him to buy a new dress for her, and that he did but the expensive cotton dress with the intricate "tibeb" decoration at its hem did not impress her. He went to the village witch doctor who gave him an amulet to wear against the "betagn" spirit that poisons the love between couples. The amulet did not work either. His wife remained distant and refused to tell him what was wrong.

He found out why by accident, well at least he believed he did. He had gone to the cattle market as usual intending to sell a few goats and to stay there for some days. The cattle market was, however, raided by armed bandits who killed some people and made off with much of the cattle including his goats. Angered by the loss and yet happy for being alive he rushed back to his village to be with his children who were staying at his parent's hut. He reached his village late at night and unwilling to wake up the children he made his way to his own compound and hut and was approaching the door when he heard voices. His wife was talking. A male voice replied. His wife giggled aloud like he had not heard her do for so long. The male voice spoke. The hut was as usual dimly lit and as he let the devil take over his thoughts he imagined his wife and the unidentified man in his bed. We say the devil smells all evil thoughts from afar, don't we? Here was Zewdu, frustrated and angry, annoyed by his wife and wallowing in self- pity, and who would expect the devil to leave him alone? Satan moved in with all his minions and started holding court in the boiling heart and brain of Zewdu. The poor man's first regret (he had said to himself I wish I had not come back from the cattle market) was quickly replaced by a volcanic fury at his wife. The cheat! The shermuta/the whore! And just as suddenly, he concluded that the male voice belonged to no other but to his best man.

The devil had his field day; get into the realm of juggling circumstantial evidence and prejudices and he will supply you with details and parts to give sense to the jigsaw puzzle. Take a lie to your bedroom and the truth will sleep naked on the street as people say. Open your heart to hatred and the devil moves in with his army of evil. As suddenly as the appearance of a shooting star in the sky, it dawned upon Zewdu that he had been duped from the start. The wedding night! His best man getting him drunk and his shermuta of a wife laughing and urging him on. And his blackout! The morning after and Woubet showing him the blood-smeared sheet that had covered the bed! I did not do it, of course, he raged. They tricked me. She was not even a virgin and she and his best man, lovers for long, had smeared a sheep's blood on the sheet and she had shown him and he, the fool, had believed he had taken her virginity.

He could have gone into the hut and found out the truth, but no. The devil had him in his grip and was driving him into the dark and fetid hole of self- pity and revenge. He was so consumed by hate and doubt that he considered for a while that even his children might not actually be his. He left his compound and slept in the forest nearby, fired by hate, unaware of the cold. In the morning, he made his way to his house and his cold wife to whom he made an effort to show the usual calm face and not the hate ravaged one. He went over to his parents and passed the day playing with his children who, he was happy to note and believe, looked like him and even smiled like him.

It was a few days later that he got the chance to do what he was planning to do. It was in fact his best man, the secret lover of his wife, who came up with the idea of the hunting trip. It was a great honor to kill a lion, it was not like now when every wimp of an adolescent boy can have his ears pierced and wear an earring. In those days a man can wear an earring only if he had killed a lion. The best man suggested that they both go to hunt a pride of lions that had killed many a cow and a bull in their village. Usually, more than two people hunted for a lion but the best man suggested that if the two of them can kill even one lion by themselves their honor and prestige would be greater. Zewdu agreed readily and ordered his wife to prepare them some 'dirkosh' and 'quanta', you know, dry rations. He noted that she looked relieved and happy as she prepared what he had asked. A few days later the two men left their village in search of the lions. The wild animals were at a half- day walking distance from the village in a forest that they both knew well. Both Zewdu and the best man were armed with Lee-Enfield 303 bolt rifles, the ones we call "guande". Hunting wild animals with automatic rifles was considered cowardly in their area.

By late afternoon they had found the pride of lions sleeping and lounging in the shade of a big zigba tree. Zewdu and his best man were on top of a small hill and looking down at the lions.

"There they are," the best man whispered excitedly, lying on his stomach and looking down. "We can get at least one or two if we do it right." They were both hunters and knew attacking a pride of lions with just two people was a very dangerous undertaking. Lions do not ran away like rabbits or today's city folks at the sound of a shot.

"Yes," agreed Zewdu, adding, "it is difficult to do it from here. Leave your gun here and scout for a better place."

The best man left his gun and slithered softly away. When he came back after a while he saw Zewdu had moved away from the edge of the hill and was carrying his rifle slung over his shoulder. The rifle of Zewdu was pointing at the best man but the latter did not notice.

"I have found a better place," he said softly. "We cannot miss them from there and if the worst comes we can also escape easily."

Zewdu raised his rifle and aimed it at the best man.

"What is it? What are you doing?" The best man sounded more amused than scared.

"What is it, you ask?" Zewdu let the hate take control. "You and my whore of a wife! I know what you have been doing. You brought me here to kill me didn't you?"

"What the hell are you talking about?" The best man looked shocked. "Why do you insult your loving wife? Why do you utter nonsense about killing you?"

But Zewdu was past beyond reasoning. He had no patience to listen. "You betrayed my trust," he shouted at his best man. "Not only did you take my wife but you plotted with her to kill me. Who came up with sudden suggestion to go on a hunting trip? You or your lover, my so- called wife? Was the plan to shoot me or to let the lions do the job?"

"Are you crazy, my friend," the best man protested. "I never slept with your wife, never betrayed you or planned to kill you. What has gotten into you?"

Zewdu was possessed by the devil of hate and murder to whom he had handed over his ears and all reasoning power.. He forced his friend to the edge of the hill and shoved him down with the butt of the rifle to fall onto the pride of lions and as you know lions, like our rulers, are never fed enough to refuse an offering.

Satisfied like most people who let the devil take possession of them to commit what they call vengeance but is most of the time plain murder, Zewdu returned to his village. It was night when he reached his compound and the hut. He was near the door when he heard voices. The voice of his wife and that of a man, which he realized with shock, was the same male voice he had heard before and had concluded belonged to the best man. The door opened and the man came out.

"Ah, it is you Zewdu," said the witch doctor. "I have been sprinkling anointment on your wife and the walls to get rid of the bad spirits. I was here last week too,

"To tell you the truth," added the witch doctor pulling Zewdu aside, "your wife was told by someone I will not name that you had a mistress at the cattle market."

"Your voice...?" stammered Zewdu.

"My voice?"

"It sounds like my Mize's." My best man's.

"You too?" said the witch doctor. "Many have told me the same thing. Anyway your wife seems to be now convinced you are loyal to her. Try to make it up with her anyways."

The witch doctor left. And Zewdu did not go into the hut to meet his wife. He could not face her; he felt he did not deserve to see her or his children ever again. He left too. Far from the village, and to the City. One more murderer in hiding in a City that keeps criminals in palaces and big villas. He had brought his conscience with him and he was to have no peace. He never went back to his wife; never saw his children again. That was his punishment. Many a time he had thought of killing himself but he had concluded that it would be an easy way out and discarded it. He became a coolie and then joined the underground movement as a means of atonement for his sins. To die for others. But he never found internal peace. Every night the face of the best man came to haunt him. I suspect it was only while he was dying, sacrificing himself to protect others, that he might have seen the face of the best man smiling at him and extending his hands in a welcome."

Neither Misikir nor Tamrat asked Matteos how he came across the story. The devil, they knew, haunted the details.

Of Dreams And Death

*I*t was years later, after two big famines had killed thousands and devastated the land, after the sound of gunfire had become a distant memory and after countless scorching suns had set in behind the depressingly barren hills that surround the City, that the dreams begun.

Allah knew that he, Ali "Tshombe", was no dreamer. On the contrary, he was very much a realistic man, a hands-on no nonsense fellow who shunned theories, fancy thoughts and the cinema. He was blacker than most and had thick lips which earned him the "Tshombe" nickname (after the late Congolese politician Moise Tshombe) from his prejudiced fellow countrymen who would otherwise never readily admit that they have a bias against their own color. Thick set and short, he had no illusion that the fair ladies would swoon at the sight of him, no. He knew his place, he took fate as it was handed to him, praised Allah and tried to give some warmth to a life that had all the promise of longevity as the life span of a fly. Inconspicuous and quiet, he had survived the tumults of the military regime and he was convinced that it was to his capacity to be inconspicuous that none of the contending forces, which were tearing at one another, approached to recruit him. He was a speck on the wall, a bed bug in an abandoned hut, there but unseen.

At thirty three, he was already feeling more than old, as if he had over-lived his sunset years and occupied the space that should have been left for others. Perpetual gloom was etched on his face and like a voyager on a long unknown trek he felt lost every inch of the way but he was unruffled by it all as he searched for nothing and expected to find nothing. Living was a day to day existence, Allah's will, a burden for sure but not in his power to end or change. He expected no windfall or luck and was not disappointed when none came his way.

The dreams haunted him. He was disturbed not only by their content but also because it was unusual for him to dream so often. He could not recall when he had ever dreamt in the past and was convinced that he had never had a dream. Eyes open or eyes closed, never. He was a loner, unmarried and dealing with his urges, when they did come to him occasionally, by paying the professionals who, (at least most of them), did not mind his looks so long as his money had the right color or weight.

Even years later, he was able to recall the first dream in vivid details, as if it was a scene he had actually witnessed. There was the open jeep with the mounted machine gun (what was called 'Kuami Teteri', the regime's real representative), much like the "Technicals" they have now in Somalia, and armed soldiers carrying AK-47s and looking fierce. The jeep was accelerating fast to reach him. Two young boys playing at wrestling on the side of the street. The jeep approaches, the young boys stop playing and from inside their pockets they take out round things they hurl at the jeep. The explosion is deafening and he falls on his stomach. A severed leg flies through the air and lands near him, foot still in an army boot. All around him people are running scared, the two young boys have disappeared and the jeep is a mangled ruin. He tries to rise up and flee and couldn't. Damp with sweat he wakes up.

The second dream that always followed the first was also clear in his mind. The boys who threw the bombs come to him. He is in a big hole much like the underground prison holes favored by the present government. The younger of the two boys talks first.

"It is quite routine," he says.

"Boringly normal," adds the other.

"Something that had to be done," says the first.

"Nothing special," says the other.

He wants so much to tell them that they should be in school and not in the street throwing grenades and killing people but his tongue feels as dead as the heart of a dictator and refuses to move.

"Maybe you feel sorry for the soldiers," says the first boy provocatively. "Maybe you would have preferred to see us die instead".

He wants to tell them that he did not want to see anyone of them dead, that the country is for all of them but his tongue dies on him.

"Maybe you are one of those who preach to the poor to live and die meekly," says the other boy. And at his point the two boys bow out of his dream to be replaced by an old crumpled woman with a long sword. When she opens her mouth he sees her inside is on fire. He notes she smells like freshly dug soil. He wants to ask her if she was death coming to take him away but he is unable to utter a word. She spits at him and his shirt is drenched with foul smelling blood. The old lady leaves to be replaced by severed and floating heads, all asking him to give them his body. "You don't need it," they scream at him. In the end a spitting image of himself appears and refuses to talk to him at all. As he desperately tries to talk to himself, he wakes up drenched in sweat and frustrated.

His third dream, the one which came to him once a week, cast him as an unborn child, trying to swim inside his mother's womb and yet fully aware that he had never learnt to swim, that he was not even born. Gripped by terror at the possibility of dying by drowning, he tears at his mother's inside to cling to something and survive. In the process, he murders his own mother and sinks drowning. And he wakes up gasping.

Ali "Tshombe" was not a man to be unduly disturbed by dreams. He would have said bismillahi and went on with his life but the problem was that the dreams haunted him to the point that he started to get scared of sleeping at night since the dreams only came to haunt him at night. The moment his eyes close the dreams assailed him. He slept less and less and started to pass nights without sleeping even for a few minutes. Tired during the day, he started sleeping at his workplace and it was not long before his boss dismissed him. He stayed put in his home, afraid to sleep during the night, dozing off during the day, ill fed, unshaven. He stopped going to the mosque and since he had hardly anyone he could call a friend no one bothered enough to visit him. Ali "Tshombe" was convinced that Allah was displeased by him and was punishing him in this manner. He resolved to accept the punishment.

Many weeks later, neighbors who were disturbed by the smell broke into his house and found his dead and inflated body. He had exhausted and starved himself to death.

Poor Ali Tshombe, said most. Such a quiet and strong bodied man, they all agreed. None of them knew that dreams had killed him much like the young victims of the repressive government. Ali Tshombe was buried and three dreams continued to float in the district for long looking for a new victim.

The Man With Another Face

Not many people know the real reason why witch doctors and magicians in Ethiopia have gone underground and are plying their trade clandestinely. The reason is just one man. Here is how it all happened.

He was no ordinary man, no. He was the Prime Minister of the impoverished country, a coward perceived as the strongest man in the nation of seventy plus million people, the man all men feared and, he hoped, all women desired. He had passed years in the jungle as a leading member of a guerrilla organization and though he had cleverly kept away from the frontlines and taken part in a battle only once (he fled and was almost executed for cowardice), he paraded as a tested and veteran guerrilla. A verbose man, he actually came across as a vulgar street- smart political con man that liked to parade as a

seasoned political strategist or war commander. He had a
whore of an ego but he was realistic enough to know that his
colleagues and the people at large laughed at his posturing.

It was a Wednesday morning in the month of April when
he woke up alone in his bed (his business minded wife had
given him two children and long ago stopped sharing a bed
with him) and dragged his plump body to the sumptuous
bathroom of the Palace. The bathroom was full of mirrors and
the moment he entered he was confronted by the image of the
former dictator Mengistu Haile Mariam. Ordinarily a coward,
he fainted outright. When he came to, he hesitantly rose to
confront the mirrors and there it, nay he, was staring back at
him. He knew he was alone. He touched his face. It was now
the face of Mengistu Maile Mariam the brutal dictator who
ruined the country and fled to Zimbabwe. Drenched in sweat,
he stared at his, no, Mengistu's face. What had happened
overnight? Had one of his enemies drugged him and had his
face changed? He realized quick enough that this was not
really the case. He was staring at his face in the mirror when
his wife suddenly entered the bathroom.

"Oh, you are finally awake," she said to him moving past
him to the golden sink.

"Yes," he said softly, happy to hear his own voice,
unchanged. He turned his back to her and moved out but she
followed him.

"What's wrong with you?" she asked. "You have this
anxious face. Are you feeling sick again?"

He smoked and drank in excess and had many ailments that
she knew about but were kept secret from the people lest they
consider him weak and get tempted to rebel.

"I am fine," he told her. "Do you find me different?"

"No but you have this attitude." She looked at him and
added: "I am going to my office. I will call you later." And she
left. As soon as she had gone he rushed back to the bathroom
and stared into the mirrors. The same face! Mengistu Haile
Mariam was staring back at him.

His face etched in desperation he went back to the bedroom

and picked the blue phone.

"Mulugeta?"

"Yes sir." Mulugeta knew his master's voice. He was the longtime friend and advisor of the Prime Minister. They both hailed from the same street in a northern town.

"Come over to my bedroom." Mulugeta slept in the Western Wing of the Palace and it did not take him long to knock at the bedroom door of the Prime Minister.

"Come in," said the PM.

Mulugeta came in and bowed respectfully.

"What do you see?" shrieked the PM with a desperate tone. "My face."

"Your face?"

"Has it changed? Is it the same?"

Mulugeta wore his confusion on his ghoulish face.

"We all change," he said diplomatically. "The lean and hungry look we had in the forest is long gone. Time flies."

"I am not asking you to state the obvious," said the irritated PM his lips curled in disgust. "Is my face mine?"

Mulugeta was ready to admit that even his own face belonged to the powerful and capricious PM. "Of course it is your face", he said instead.

"No change?"

"No change."

"How come then I see Mengistu's ugly face in the mirror?"

"Mengistu?" Mulugeta could not hide his surprise. "The dictator? The butcher?"

"The same," wailed the PM. "The dog who is enjoying exile in Harare."

"You look your same old self to me," said Mulugeta. "Nothing can make you look like that fascist."

The Prime Minister shuffled back to the bathroom and saw the same face of Mengistu in the mirror. He summoned Mulugeta to come and see which Mulugeta did.

"I see your face," said Mulugeta.

"I see Mengistu," said the PM.

"Is this a conscience thing?" asked Mulugeta boldly.

"Nonsense," said the PM who had long ago parted with his ever- tiny conscience. "He had a face which said no long before you asked him anything. Not like mine."

Mulugeta chose to be silent.

"Not that I resemble him in any way," said the PM moving back to his big bedroom and sinking into a Louis XIV imitation-gold chair. "He was a dictator."

Mulugeta, who knew that most people also called the PM a dictator, communed with his own silence.

"If my act does not resemble his, why should my face change to his?"

Mulugeta dared to flirt with danger. "Could it be magic?" he asked knowing full well that the PM, for all his anti-left rhetoric to please the Americans, still fancied himself as a die hard communist of the Albanian- Stalinist mold.

"Magic? What magic?"

In for the festivities, in for the mourning-- Mulugeta pressed on. "You know the dark and mysterious world of the witch doctors of the north west. They are a mischievous and devilish lot who pee on churches and make pacts with the devil. Do you remember their attempt to free the late Emperor from Mengistu's prison by turning him into a mouse? Mengistu had all mice in the prison compound trapped and burnt. Some were even shot. He did not leave anything to chance. If you see Mengistu's detested face in the mirror instead of yours it can only be a "mezewir" cast on you by some notorious wizard."

"Who?"

"We can search and find out," proposed Mulugeta.

And so, the hunt begun all over the country. Witch doctors and exorcists, magicians and wizards were hunted. Many were netted and all denied ever having cast the "mezewir", change of appearance, spell on the PM. Famous wizards from the PM's own home region were summoned to change the effects of the "mezewir" but none were able to do so. The prisons filled up with the witch doctors of the north- west, the east, the west and the central parts of the country much as the concentration camps were filled with political prisoners from the same areas. The PM found no solace in all this. Mengistu's face confronted him every time in the mirror. And that was why the decree that made everyone in the world laugh emanated from the palace in Ethiopia: break all mirrors! Anyone caught with a mirror was to be considered a counter revolutionary and anti-peace dissident. From Washington, where self declared democrats routinely praise dictators, came the admiring support to this act: "the money saved from buying mirrors imported from China, where slave labor is used, can be channeled into combating famine!"

If you meet Ethiopians who look unwashed or are passing clandestine hours in front of a mirror, please remember that they have been denied the right to look at a mirror and see themselves.

The Trip Within

From the cold heights of the hills of Entoto, he looked down at his City and saw the desolation and destruction that had been brought on it. Not one building stood, smoldering fire sent dark clouds up to the skies; it looked as if the punishment of Sodom and Gomorrah had been visited upon the City of his birth.

He rushed down with the speed of a shooting star and found himself right in the Mercato that had been before an overcrowded and vibrant part of the sprawling City. There was nobody in sight and everything had fallen down, burnt down, been torn apart. Tears welled up in his eyes. Where was I while my City got destroyed, he wailed unto himself. His first thought was of Somalia but he soon discarded that. The perennial enemy of his country had been torn apart by its own inter clan war and was in no position to invade and damage anyone. More than that, the City was home to thousands of Somalis who fled from their clan war and they would not destroy their own refuge. He thought of Eritrea, a separate country now and with much rancor and feeling of vengeance towards his country but then again it was incapable of wreaking such havoc so far from its own borders.

The old man appeared from the ruins on the right. He was naked from the waist up, emaciated, long white beard cascading down to his chest. He carried a long pole much like the "mequamia", the long wooden pole favored by nuns and used as a support by the old during the three hours mass service. He was barefoot and wearing tattered green shorts.

He did not even greet the old man but asked: "What on earth happened?" in a hysterical voice.

"You should know," said the old man in a baritone and vigorous voice that should have belonged to a much younger person. "Look," he ordered.

And he looked.

He saw a man sitting on a golden throne; his sight was blurred and much as he squinted he could not see the face of the man. The man on the throne waved a wand and right in front of him the City opened up, as he knew it, with new and tall buildings vying for space with slums and cardboard shacks and roadside plastic shelters. A donkey straggled up a steep street with blood dripping from its behind in the process of a birth to come soon. A boy with an enormous head and just one eye extended a hand to beg. Thousands of mutilated people, young and old, raised their hands imploringly. On a side street, armed soldiers shot dead scores of people lined against the wall. As soon as the dead got removed, another batch got lined up against the wall and the soldiers executed these too and on it went continuously. On another street, he could see a big store-like hall, dirt floor, and filled by more than three hundred people. They were almost all young but there were also a few old men and women. All were on the floor, many were bleeding, some were moaning in pain. On the stage, there were five young and middle-aged men strutting about with whips, they were all armed with pistols and Kalashnikov rifles. On the table on the stage there was a naked girl tied by a rope. Her whole body was covered with blood. The armed men flogged her and they roared with laughter with every blood they drew from her bruised body. The hundreds in the hall sang, "how nice to see/a counter revolutionary bleed/ how nice to watch/this anti peace getting sliced". The torturers untie the girl and throw her inert body unto the stone floor of the hall. They call a young boy to come foreword and he does so trembling. He is tied in turn and they use various instruments to cut off his flesh and to torture him viciously. Two of the armed people call ten people to the foot of the stage and they herd them out of the hall to shoot them in cold blood just outside. More armed men came in bringing more prisoners and the hall was filling up. The torturers do an "iskista" dance at the sight of more bodies to play with.

And suddenly, the man on the throne moves his wand and the City disappears to be replaced by a sprawling field filled with dead bodies piled one on top of the other. The smell assails him and he gags. Both the old man and the man on the throne laugh at him.

"Don't tell me you never saw so many dead bodies," says the old man.

He hesitates. "No," he chooses to reply.

"No?" The old man shakes his head in amazement. "Where were you when mutilated bodies were thrown all over the streets? Where were you when the morgue was full of dead youngsters?"

He was in the City, no doubt.

"You had eyes but did not see," said the old man.

"It did not concern me," he argued. "Am I my brother's keeper?"

"How is that? You lived in the City; you were a citizen, no? How could it not concern you when the flowers of the nation got tortured and killed just because they dared to dream."

"Know thy place, says the Lord," he quoted seeking a refuge. "If you contest the powers that be, it is only to be expected that they will retaliate."

"Now you see why the City got destroyed? Because

indifferent people like you embraced their cowardice and made it possible for other cowards in power to stamp out any notion of courage and decency. Truth was an outcast because your mistress was falsehood."

Look, ordered the old man again. And he looked.

Bullets were tracing lines on the sky, the canons roared. From the mountain afar, armed men wearing tattered khaki shirts and shorts advanced, shooting from the hip their automatic weapons, assaulting the fortress defended by the government soldiers. Many fell on the way but the advance did not stop. He looked harder and saw that the assaulting force was made up of very young boys and girls, not many of them more than fourteen.

"But they are children," he heard himself say.

"What do you expect?" countered the old man. "The likes of you refused to fight for your own country. Children had to die in your place. Look," ordered the old man.

And he looked and saw the mountains of his country drenched with blood and covered by rotting corpses.

"What did you do then?" the old man asked.

Look, said the old man again. And he saw the Kerchiele and other prisons filled by young and old alike. He saw policemen beating up on them, he saw the hangman executing scores and in the concentration camps he saw prisoners dying from diseases and mistreatment. And he saw the streets of the City as he had never seen it before: babies abandoned on garbage dumps, children begging and sleeping on the streets, preteen girls being raped by officials, former soldiers now destitute and turned into beggars, informers cocking their ears, police beating up newspaper vendors, AIDS victims dying abandoned, sane people thrown into mental asylums, shackled and tortured by electrodes, elderly and young women carrying loads and sweating up steep streets, hungry children wailing endlessly, naked prisoners in underground holes, and the rich driving by in their Cobra Land Cruisers, jeeps and Mercedes-Benzs carrying their plump bodies and tiny hearts to luxurious homes and hotels.

"Where were you?" the old man asked again. "Where were you when the youth fled the City and the country and mothers went to church not to pray for life but for an early death and deliverance? When they all prayed to God 'finish us off before we see such deaths'? "

He saw thousands of people fleeing from Wellega and Arabgugu as monsters, with fiery tongues, chased them. He saw men and women being thrown down the Bedeno cliffs by crazed dwarfs who had "HATE!" tattooed on their foreheads. And he watched as government soldiers shot dead innocent people at the Areka market and Awassa and machine-gunned people praying at the Adebabye Iyesus Church and the Anwar mosque. He saw dead bodies everywhere and all of a sudden he saw many zombie-like people walking around the destroyed City. Naked, eyes vacant, dried-up bodies as if their blood had been sucked dry by a modern day Buda or evil eye. And he saw that they had all his face.

"What?" he exclaimed in shock.

"You were one of the living dead," said the old man. "You all destroyed the City. You were given life but you preferred to go through life like a zombie controlled by evil spirits."

Look said the old man and he disappeared from sight.

And he looked and saw thousands of people descend on the city like locusts from the sky and they tore every building down. All the thousands looked like him and then their faces and bodies merged, came together and landed on the throne that was no longer golden but drenched in blood. And on the throne, he saw now clearly, sat no one else but himself.

He awoke suddenly from his nightmare and immediately vowed never to eat a heavy supper of raw meat that always gave him indigestion and bad dreams. As he later drove expensive Pajero to work, he was immersed in the Elton John song coming from his CD player and did not see the half-naked young girls and boys on the street extending their hands and begging him for some coins.

The Sheratonians

"He is a heavyweight in the internet," said Roman with a trace of irritation in her voice. "How could you not know him? He wrote the series of articles in the discussion network on 'The Psychological Need for Famine in the Mindset of the Ordinary Ethiopian'."

Roman ("please call me Romy") took a sip from her Martini Dry and looked disapprovingly at her table companion. She was short, earth-eyed, slim but bosomy, with a round face covered by excessive make-up.

"You exaggerate Romy," said Tadesse ("please call me Teddy "). "I hardly ever connect to these Internet forums. Read one read all, boring to the core. I hate pseudo intellectuals and hyphenated Ethiopians."

If Roman call me Romy was a graduate of the City's one and only Lycee and a full fledged Francophone who had started and never finished her university studies in Grenoble, France, Tadesse, call me Teddy, was a product of a non descript college in South Western USA where all students necessarily graduated with a degree and none failed to make it, a college much like the ex-Lumumba University in Moscow to which many Third World intellectuals had been sent for "political" degrees.

"The hyphenated fools," went on Teddy, "are neither Ethiopian nor American and in the description of themselves as Ethio-Americans they divide their very soul into confusion. Hence, their incomprehensible articles over the internet."

"They are no more hyphenated than us," said Romy. "We are intellos in a country of crass illiterates and therefore anomalies quoi".

Tadesse (call me "Teddy"), who had a rasping voice, was a well-built middle aged man whose pallid and thick lips and beady eyes contrasted with a bulbous nose in a beefy face. He usually drank Chivas Regal whisky and this time too, though it was not yet six pm ("flag lowering time" as it is said to denote also the beginning of the daily 'decent' alcohol drinking time), he had already entered his own happy hour by consuming three doubles. Romy and Tadesse were seated at their usual table at the far corner of the Blue Room of the bar in the exclusive Sheraton Hotel. This was their usual haunt be it morning, afternoon or night.

"It is not related to being an intellectual actually," said Teddy lighting up yet another cigarette. "It is dislocation really. The average Ethio-American is a peasant at his core, a raw-meat consuming unchanged Abyssinian with a veneer of the American, the gun worshipping West. He calls his children Gaby, Suzy and," here Teddy smiled, "and even Teddy, and yet wants to act the peasant father and to beat them up to install discipline in them. He is neither at home there nor at home here."

"What about us then? We are fine here. We are Ethiopians though not so mundane or pedestrian like the masses out there in the stinking streets".

"Well, we are Ethiopians in our own way," said Teddy. "We are aliens in our own City. Why do you think we congregate together here in this luxurious hotel that has little of

Ethiopia to it?"

Romy shrugged and sipped her Martini. The Blue Room was filling up, she noticed. Young nouveau riches who obviously had the money but not the culture to be dressed properly. Young pretty women mesmerizing their elderly companions with their soft brown eyes and studied grace. Young high class whores trying to look anything but, sitting with their cover boys, that is the boys paid to accompany them into the Sheraton since unaccompanied girls can be turned away. Experienced Greek and Arab prostitutes smoking long filter tipped cigarettes and trying to look unapproachable. Government officials who were only yesterday uncouth peasant guerrillas and low level clerks sipping expensive cognac and whisky and fidgeting uncomfortably while effortlessly succeeding to make the Armani and Saville Row suits they wore look unsightly. Over at one corner sat a group of pot-bellied and skeletal thin men trying to look inconspicuous while almost everyone knew they were from the political police. Romy sighed content at the usual scene.

"Do you see that owl there?" asked Romy signaling with her head towards a thin, tall and pretty girl about to sit in a chair being pulled back for her by a fat man in a tight fitting black three pieces suit. Teddy nodded.

"A pathetic sight, isn't she?" went on Romy venomously. "Three children from three different men, all the kids sent back to her mother in some rural stink hole. She has yet to finish high school but she pretends to be an intellectual of the highest caliber. Merde."

"Why is she important?" asked Tadesse.

"Well, her present husband—not this frog accompanying her—is from the elite group, some say even close to the main Man, you know, the PM. You remember the Ogaden fellow who was the bedroom carpet for the PM? Some say her husband has replaced him".

"Maybe the big fellow is bedding her," said Tadesse with a smile. Romy looked fearfully around her.

"Be careful of what you say," she warned. "Those four

there are spies and it is not only the Ghion that is bugged. To come to your point though, the PM's wife has been bitching about lack of such attention from him though I don't think he is servicing this ugly bird."

"I find her pretty actually," said Tadesse provocatively.

"I didn't expect any different. For men like you, beauty is a straight nose and a slim body well wrapped in a Lacroix smelling of Dior perfumes."

Teddy refrained from telling Romy she was almost defining herself.

"Did you see Tefera over there? He hardly ever greets us anymore," Romy complained.

"Why should he? He may have repented or even betrayed and joined the present government but he still thinks we are the same reactionaries we were before."

"Talk of yourself," said Romy lighting a cigarette. "These so called Revos who have repented, what moral ground have they to look down upon us? Tefera claims he was a member of the urban armed-squad of one group or the other at the time but those who know him well say he is just posturing. In fact, he was jailed only briefly and then again by mistake and he was released while others were shot. Muktar knows his story very well."

"Those who fought at that time, wouldn't you say they have at least done something anyway no matter if they stayed on or not."

"You should not begin what you will not take to the end," said Romy. "A prayer you don't finish brings damnation upon you. You don't catch a tiger's tail and once you do you should never let go. I never agreed with their leftist prattle but shame on those who enter the tiger's den and flee out with their trousers soiled. Those who continued are better than them though I hardly agree with their political views."

"You are hard and contradictory," observed Tadesse. "How can you say they are wrong in their views and admire their doggedly pursuing their goal?"

"No, realistic. You can't have it both ways. Either you live according to your principles or you make just living your principle like us. And you can admire someone's courage and steadfastness even when you disagree with him. L'audace, de l'audace as the French say."

"Yet, we can also be faulted in the same way," said Tadesse. "We softly criticize the government, we claim to be above it all, don't we? And yet we bow and live this life of ours which the millions cannot imagine let alone have."

"And what is wrong with that, my dear Teddy? Our rulers have always been crass but ruthless brutes. We have to adjust, play along with them. It is a doomed country. C'est la vie."

"I wonder sometimes if we are part of her problem, this poor country of ours," said Teddy.

"Look at those five over there," Romy said signaling with her head to the left. "All five have their cellular phones on the table. Showing off. Let one ring and all five will pick it up and try to talk. Shame! I do hate 'arrivists' and their pathetic attempt to look modern."

"It is their time," said Teddy . "What Warhol said was fifteen minutes of fame."

"They wouldn't know a Warhol from a bloody hole," snapped Romy. "Crude peasants pretending to be sophisticated. Have you noticed that none of them ever order caviar, shrimp or Lobster. The most they can do is order a steak tartare, as good as having a 'kitfo' or the raw meat they are comfortable with."

"They are late," said Teddy changing the subject.

Theirs was a group of six who sat every evening at this table drinking and smoking, eating Belugia caviar and other aperitifs imported from France and Italy, and back- biting their friends and enemies alike and insulting the "unwashed masses", and just chilling as Teddy liked to say. Aside from Romy and Teddy, there was Abiyou, a tall, emaciated and highly paid lawyer who had done his studies in Canada and whose rich father had been killed by the former military regime, leaving him with an ocean -deep hatred against the generation that brought the Revolution. A rich man (some of the wealth inherited from the dead father who had had the foresight of opening a foreign bank account), Abiyou was consumed by his hate and always wore the pained look of a very constipated man. Like all hate consumed people, he was also boringly unoriginal, repetitive in his condemnations and facile conclusions. He liked to be called Abe as Abraham Lincoln. There was also Ijigayehu (everyone calls me Jiggy) with her delicate face and features (straight nose, inviting lips, wide brown eyes and melon breasts) that the City dwellers defined as aristocratic and therefore beautiful. Ijigayehu was not as highly educated as the others but she had also a very rich father who had managed to survive the Revolution and to betroth his daughter to a foreign educated engineer with his own building firm and useful connections within the government. Her rich husband never knew she was unfaithful to him and thus did not cut her off his will and, when he died of a sudden stroke, she inherited his wealth and took up the task of living every day as the last after packing off her two sons to the USA to finish their education. Alone and a non-grieving widow, a creature that fans trouble as people say, she boasted of having "tasted" or bedded down most of the City's worthwhile bachelors and adulterous husbands. The other member of the group was Eskinder ("please call me Doctor Alex, always doctor, please"), a short and flabby university professor who sported a Trotsky goatee and had a predatory expression on his rat-like face. Dr. Alex was once a radical intellectual who out shone many a dope smoking radical in the Californian university campuses (where he taught after finishing his studies at Harvard), joined a few ML groups, stayed close to the Black Panthers (he liked to recount tall tales of his close cooperation with Panther leaders Huey Newton and Bobby Seale), boasted of having clandestine contacts even with the Weathermen group and had really penned a number of Marxist articles that for a while influenced the ideological choice of the youth movement in his own country. As fate would have it, Dr. Alex concentrated more on partying than on party politics and the Movement in his country left him in the lurch, condemning him as a bitter revisionist, a has been, and worse of all, an opportunist. Dr. Alex withdrew to his drugs, alcohol and women (he never lacked any of the three) and when his health condition threatened to deteriorate to a dangerous level he returned to the country after more than two decades of self imposed exile and became the behind the scene political advisor of the new rulers in addition to teaching at the run down university in the City. If Dr. Alex kept his radical politics at the verbal level and never engaged in any actual act of protest, the last member of the Sheraton group, Muktar, had been an active member of the very militant and radical underground group that, in the seventies, battled against military rule in the cities and rural jungles. Muktar left first year university studies to join the underground movement when not being a member of this group was considered as swimming against the current and thus not safe. To be fair to Muktar, he did believe he had some radical ideals and principles but he was, as most said later on, just not married to them. A wife goes, a wife comes, she is not irreplaceable like your mother, say the people. When situations change and you are called up to die for your principles remember a coward bends, betrays, does a Judas and a Peter on all and lives on for his mother, as Muktar has often repeated to himself. When the Red Terror begun, he betrayed his comrades and saved his life. He joined the government party, finished his studies, became a business man, engaged in the illegal trade called "air by air", became rich and when the new government came he expressed his support to the new rulers by publicly re-condemning his old organization and vowing loyalty to the "new democratic order". The new rulers had made him head of one of the State owned companies and he was making more money openly and much more on the side.

The Sheraton Six shared some common prejudices and visceral hatreds and thus made sure their friendship would last much like the friendship of two travelers who are afraid of wild animals and are forced to walk through the jungle together. They would have never admitted it publicly but they were all people embittered by their experiences and failings. Romy had lost a would- be husband to her younger and more beautiful sister who left with the catch (a French doctor) to Paris and to a life, at least Romy assumed, of decadent French opulence. Abiyou was a rich and successful lawyer consumed by hate and more afflicted by the secret burden he had to carry and rendered him less of a man than any homeless and miserable Getachew or Hailu in the homophobe country. Teddy was a chain- smoking alcoholic tolerated by most because he was a good conversationalist and (even though now washed out) an "intello" from the great United States of America no matter if he graduated from a small and non- prestigious university. Teddy doubled also as a well paid- informer to the new government while Dr. Alex was an intellectual of stature (or so many believed), an ugly man but with that "mother me" trait which never failed to catch a pretty bird, and yet a miserable and pitiful man who desperately envied the men of action who dared to stand up and die for their principles. People hated Dr. Alex because he publicly defended the repressive government and this had added to his chagrin and frustration, to his self-loathing and round the clock state of tipsiness. Like the street boys who sniffed at rags soaked in petrol or glue to intoxicate themselves and not to feel the pain of their hunger and daily misery, Dr. Alex also soaked his body in alcohol almost around the clock (his students enjoyed hearing him lecture in a slurred voice) and drowned his ever dwindling conscience. Ijigayehu was adequately rich, still good looking enough to get any man to bed but inside herself she had always felt like an uneducated whore and felt some importance only when she joined her intellectual friends in the Sheraton or heard the orgasmic screams of many a proud man lured to her bed. Stinking beings stick and trek together, as people say. The Sheraton Six stank but none of them had the nose for the smell they exuded and thus they stuck together. As the City folk say: stink is good company to stink or as the ancestors said wisely ' for the smelly breath God will provide the blocked nose'.

It was eight o'clock and in the dining hall the white- gloved waiters in their finely embroidered uniforms were serving the rich and powerful and the not so rich and not so powerful customers seated around tables lit by colored candles in silver candle bars. There was every thing of your choice served on Limoges china, from Beluga caviar to truffles, from lobster and fresh asparagus to Pate de foie gras to steak tartare. But the six were seated at their usual table in the Blue Room reserved for the hard drinkers. Romy tried to restate her annoyance at Teddy's ignorance.

"Can you imagine?" she said rolling her eyes. "Teddy did not even know the internet heavy weight, the very man who explained to the masses why they need periodic famine to deal with their psyche and over population."

"What a shame," said Dr. Alex with a mocking smile. "Leave Teddy alone, Romy. The pseudo intellectual you refer to is but a fake. In my days we called the likes of him half-baked." He took a big sip from his whisky glass. "The people need famine as much as they need lice and fleas."

Teddy puffed at his cigarette and said: "I say again that the hyphenated Ethiopian is an anomaly. Being Ethiopian is already a result of so many ethnical hyphenations and fusions—add to it American and confusion reigns."

Muktar joined in with a squeaky voice. "The masses need law and order. In the past, we wasted our lives for them and what did we get in return? They applauded the soldiers and joined them to kill us poor fools struggling for what we imagined was going to be their liberation. The premise that slaves want to be free is flawed."

"Ever the reactionary," mocked Roman. "No one is as bitter as a defrocked priest or a revolutionary who has lost his ideals."

"Beware of the whore who becomes a nun," Teddy interjected with a smile.

"To come back to the issue though", went on Romy, "I cannot imagine how people can live without the Internet and the chance to surf as they please. For me these days, food is not essential. I think I will die if I let a day pass without surfing."

"When I was in California I never did surf," said Dr. Alex tipsily. "Many of the starving who have no computers will not agree with you, Romy."

"The Revolution destroyed an equitable imperial system," said Abiyou. "The Emperor was a glue holding the disparate country together till those communist agitators blinded people and brought about the Revolution. All went up in smoke," he added with a sad voice. "I lost a father, the whole country lost an Emperor and peace."

A middle- aged waiter came to their table and took away the empty glasses and brought them refills. None of them noticed him. The Blue room was now full, young girls in expensive dresses and heavy make- ups drank with their male companions wearing three- piece silk suits or expensive black leather jackets. Not every rich person, nouveau or established, made it into the Blue Room. Security and class demanded that the ones allowed entry be only those in high positions of power or those associated with or vouched for by them, and high priced whores who are always found where high class power congregates. The usual customers of the Blue Room felt a bond, almost all had sold off their soul to the temporal or celestial devil, many were still selling their bodies, all were soiled by the burden of their shameful existence. Yet, entry into the Blue Room and being accepted as a regular was a status symbol like driving a Mercedes sports car, the latest costly Cobra or some other Land Cruiser or Pajero from Japan or having an admission ring to the exclusive private club to which the top ruling party officials went after midnight. Foreigners, businessmen and diplomats or just plain but well-heeled tourists, flocked also to the Blue Room.

The people referred to as the masses called the Sheraton crowd the "Sheraton Gosa", the Tribe of the Sheraton, much as the African bourgeoisie of the seventies was called the "Benzwaza" the tribe of the Mercedes Benz. In a country officially divided on ethnic grounds, the Sheraton Gosa was a

group by its own, mostly made up of those coming from the
elite group but also made up of others who had bowed to its
domination and sold themselves to it. The Sheraton Gosa was
the new parasitic bourgeoisie of the country, grotesque in its
opulence in face of the grinding poverty of the millions, cruel
in its total disregard for the dead and dying children of the
nation. It was the tribe of greed and of cruel indifference,
ensconced in its own cocoon of luxury built by Arab money,
afraid of the grim reality outside, it was soaked in expensive
French perfumes while the City stank around it, and scared of
the impending settling of debts, another Revolution, it
condemned those who refused to sell their self respect as
violent savages.

"Forget the hyphenated," said Romy with a dismissive
gesture. "Tonight we have something to discuss." She looked
affectionately at Abiyou. "Someone wants to join our group."

A look of consternation appeared on the faces of Dr. Alex
and Muktar. Ijigayehu looked expectant and surprised while
Abiyou just smiled. Teddy stared into his glass and sunk
further into his chair.

"Who is it?" asked Dr. Alex, eyes narrowed suspiciously.
"You know our rules."

Does the cat forget to drink milk?" Romy smiled fondly at
him. "He knows and fulfills all the rules."

"Informal as we are, a tight group is what we are", said
Muktar and did not notice the quizzical look cast at him by
Abiyou. "Rules and regulations are crucial. An unruly cock in
a chicken coop can cause havoc."

Teddy smiled dazedly. "A cock in any chicken coop causes
some havoc" was what he said.

Romy gestured impatiently. "He would be a plus to our
group. A new arrival right from downtown Dallas. A Ph.d in
computer science from a prestigious university, a confirmed
cynic, good vibes with the present government, well to do
parents and financially comfortable, a rising star. Divorced
from a ravishing blond years ago."

"How come other groups did not suck him in?" Dr. Alex's skepticism was carried by his tone. "I am suspicious of these new returnees. We came back in 1991 and faced the music by supporting the new government."

"He is a relative of Abiyou and wants to be with him," said Romy and Abiyou nodded.

"So you two had discussed it already," said Ijigayehu. "How old is he by the way?"

Romy smiled knowingly. "Late thirties and quite handsome. Not married at the present time and no children at all if you really want to know," she said winking at Jiggy.

"Too many groups have collapsed from the inclusion of the wrong person," went on Dr. Alex. "Our rules are clear. We need no puritan fellow for example. We all share some feelings for the you- know- whos in power but we need no aggressively and overtly political person here. We have to be careful."

And so the discussion went on up to midnight as they drank and ate (caviar, salmon, and other "aperitifs" as Romy called them) and in the end it was clear to most of them that Dr. Alex was afraid of the competition since he was the only Phd of the group. The wily Romy saved the situation at last by declaring: "Actually, his main desire to be with us stemmed from his blind admiration for Dr. Alex here. I found it excessive to be honest but when he mentions Dr. Alex's name he almost blushes. Our mentor was what he said. The Giant."

"A blushing African", Teddy mocked but no one paid attention to him.

Dr. Alex smiled with satisfaction and it only took a few minutes for him to withdraw his reserve and to approve the inclusion of the new member of the Sheraton Six-now seven-.

"There is one problem," said Abiyou. "He—by the way his name is Getachew and I call him Getty -is having a lot of difficulty to adjust to the sight of the smelly masses dirtying the City. Nauseous all the time, that's what he is, pathetic. What can he do?"

"Does he drive a car with plain glass windows? Does he frequent the streets during the day?" Dr. Alex sounded incensed. "By God, man, teach him the basics. Dark sunglasses, car with dark shaded windows, no strolling during the day, no eyes for the riffraff millions on the streets. Perfumed handkerchiefs. Basic survival technique, my man."

Dr. Alex was in that state of inebriation that usually made him venture into the philosophical with cynical and assumed nonchalance.

"There are things we can change and many others we cannot," said Dr. Alex enjoying the attention of the others. "In our younger days most of us here, me, Muktar and many others deluded ourselves by imagining another world. What was it really? We were not sure, we did not really know, but we thought we saw it bright just across the mountain, on the horizon, and we harangued the unwashed millions to accept our vision. They did not. Forget the Revolution, it was nothing but a mob event, a selfish upheaval by City dwellers wanting a pay rise. The agitators that we were saw in all this a change of historic proportions but in the end the Emperor left and his soldiers and officers sat on his throne."

"Plus ça change plus ça reste le même, say the French," said Romy. "The tomorrow many talked about was but the past in shabby clothes."

"Precisely," beamed Dr. Alex. "That is true for the whole of Africa. The dreamers died with their dreams. Nkrumah and Lumumba, take even Sankara in Burkina Faso, they are all examples of this problem of reality and dreams. The reality wins out in the end and the dreams that work are only those which start out denying to be dreams and refusing to take themselves seriously".

Ijigayehu, "everyone calls me Jiggy", who had a hard time following this and was getting visibly bored interjected at this point. She said: "Dreams are expensive and frequented by those who have nothing better to do than sleep."

They all laughed.

"To come back to my point," said Dr. Alex, "our eyes do not see the miserable thousands right outside of this marvelous hotel not because we are blind but we are convinced there is nothing worthwhile to see. Starving children are news to foreigners who shed crocodile tears, set up one NGO after another, send their unprepared and inexperienced youngsters over with huge pay and per diem allowances and make money out of the misery but the Lords of Poverty can hardly impress us. Corpses are aplenty, beggars far too many, mutilated unfortunates uncountable. You remember the big famine when the actress Liv Ullmann came over to visit a famine camp and congratulated one starved man on the beauty of his hand knitted cap? The man was dying of hunger, my God! As we say a clumsy kisser covers you with spittle. In 1984, how many Hollywood actors and media personalities had their pictures taken with starved children and about to die famine victims? It was all just one big miserable show; they never did understand the why of it all. We cannot define our fate in conjunction with the misery of others. This is not selfishness but accepting reality, dreaming the possible. If Lumumba had taken care not to provoke America and Belgium he would have lived and ruled for much more years than the shady Mobutu. Sankara would have outwitted Campaore and even our own Mengistu may have survived longer had he abandoned his radical nonsense and pro-Soviet mumbo jumbo in time."

"Siad Barre for one ," started out Abiyou but Dr. Alex cut him short.

"A short sighted tribalist!" said Dr. Alex with a spiteful voice. "He wanted to establish a Barre dynasty backed by the Merihan minority clan. He could have shared the banana or whatever else it is that they are supposed to have in that desert they call Somalia. Live and let live, let the Hargeisa Issas numb their brain to uselessness by chewing Kat twenty- four seven. No, he had to come up with an edict forbidding the sale and chewing of Kat. Unrealistic through and through. Sometimes I wonder if the real Somali has much in common with the characters you find in their famous novelist's books. We share many prejudices but their boiling point is lower than ours and much as we may boast that we have defeated them in many battles they have no need of borrowing courage from anybody. Before Barre could say "nebad" he had to flee to exile, chased by Hawiyes and Issas armed by the wily Mengistu. Take Moi instead. He bribed the opposition and was a repressive dictator but he did not rely exclusively on repression. He is the Kalenjin Machaivelli who has survived the most."

"While Somalia sunk into anarchy," added Abiyou. "The people need a powerful leader. If we had not lost the Emperor...."

"You do not build a shade for last year's rain," said Muktar. "Let the Rastas worship the old King. We should know better. I still say a dictator is bad. Perhaps a benevolent despot can work but in Africa, the spirits in the Palaces and State Houses have no idea of benevolence. They inject all power holders with intolerance and cruelty. The Emperor you admire because your father was having it nice at the time reduced three fourths of the people to serfdom, discriminated against most on the basis of ethnicity and religion."

"And what followed pray tell?" asked Abiyou with a sarcastic tone.

"The Emperor had even little cherubic boys castrated to make them guards in the inner chambers of the princesses," said Muktar ignoring Abiyou's question. "Not to talk of the children slaughtered for his protector devil in the Bishoftu lakes."

"Gossip," said Abiyou angrily. "How can you believe such nonsense? A devil in the lake! Such wild tales only dupe the whites that want to believe the worst about us. Like the wild tales of the traveler Bruce."

"Do not thousands in the this City of ours still go to witchdoctors?" Muktar gulped down his whiskey and went on: "aren't the witchdoctors getting so rich that some of them even visit our beloved Hotel here from time to time?"

"I detect a trace of the old Leftist in your diatribe against the Emperor." Abiyou said this with a serious face.

"Once a Red always a Commie," said Teddy and sucked on his cigarette. "Yet, I also say each people must have a system best fitted for it. The Emperor was neither good nor bad, he was just our destiny for those long years. Thailand thrives on child prostitution as we do so here. Gambia peddles its muscled men to elderly white women tourists. Who is to say all this is bad? After all, it is our tradition to marry off girls as young as ten years old. Why can't they be on the streets to work for themselves in the perfect spirit of the free market? If some people are hooked on drugs why can we deny poor Burma or Colombia the opportunity of supplying them for a price? Aren't we selling coffee and America and Zimbabwe tobacco, the Scots whiskey?

"Your cynicism knows no bounds," said Roman. "Our sisters are being soiled by foreign tourists at such an early age and you condone that?"

Since almost all of them knew that Romy held a grudge against foreigners ever since her French boyfriend absconded with her younger sister back to France they did not contradict her.

"Capitalism is what it is at," said Abiyou with enthusiasm. "I must also confess that I enjoy a night with young and fresh girls."

All of them, who knew that Abiyou was gay and had never raised the subject with him at all though they hoped others looked upon them as tolerant and modern, gave him what is known as the "above neck" (fake and not from the heart) smile.

The Sheratonians usually slept late and some, who avoided going to their work place most of the time, were like vampires who never saw the daylight. The Sheraton Six who were planning to be seven separated for the night at around two p.m. Dr. Alex was too drunk to drive and slept in his usual reserved room in the hotel. Teddy was driven to his Bole villa by Romy who declined his half-hearted invitation to sleep over in his house. Abiyou drove back to his desolate villa to take his frustration to his cold bed. Jiggy drove her Hyundai saloon car to a Villa in the old airport area where she woke up a certain clerk by the name of Tulu and took him back to her house for perfunctory but, for her, satisfactory sex. Muktar stayed at the Sheraton with another group made up of uneducated cadres who looked up to his assumed sophistication and wisdom.

The next evening the Sheraton Six were joined by the new member, Getachew, but surprisingly Muktar was absent.

"He did not call," Romy informed the others. "What could have happened to him?"

"Absence without notice is not tolerated," said Dr. Alex looking at the new member of the group. "What is the use of a mobile phone then?"

"Maybe he had a force majeure," said Abiyou. "It happens".

"Force majeure is the usual in our country," joked Teddy though no one joined his laugh. "What can be special?"

"If you read the dailies for one, a child born with a horn," said Jiggy. "A woman who has a cathedral beard, a monk who is an alcoholic and a virgin girl who shot dead her abductor."

"You read the gutter press?" Romy's indignation was apparent in her face. "You did not hear the PM say do not read them?"

Jiggy gave her a non- expressive smile and tactfully chose to be silent.

It was around ten pm while the group was tactfully grilling the new member about his life that the mystery of Muktar's disappearance got clarified.

The two men who came into the Blue Room stood out as would an African in a Ku Klux Klan convention. Wearing ill fitting and cheap suits and ties, crew cut and identically bullet-headed, wearing death mask faces and trying to hide their discomfort in being in such a high class environment, they were led by a waiter to the table of the Sheraton Six who fell silent and looked apprehensive as the two men approached.

The two did not show any ID but they had all the air and smell of the political police much feared by the common man and the likes of the Sheraton Seven too.

The older of the two spoke first.

"Muktar has been detained," he said in a voice that had no

tone or feeling. "He is accused of corruption and taking part in the Red Terror. He claims you know him well and can testify in his favour."

The Prime Minster was purging his own ranks by accusing his rivals of corruption and the Red Terror tag was pinned to all and sundry who fell out with him.

"Muktar?" Abiyou tried to project a confused face.

"Yes, Muktar," answered the younger security agent. "He is part of your group. We know."

We know! This was the phrase most feared by the Nation. Security and police officers banging at your door in the middle of the night or long before dawn and before beggars had relieved themselves, torturers piercing your skin with needles or hanging a sand-filled bottle over your privates, all saying ominously We Know. What do they know? What don't they know? Did they even need to know? It was all useless and futile. The Sheraton Seven, now six, maintained the silence of the Waldiba monastery where the vow of silence is mostly in vigor.

"He does come to spend the evening with us," said Dr. Alex. "We just talk academia, you know."

The two agents did not but they saved face by their silence.

"He was always claiming he had money from an inheritance," said Abiyou opening the door for his friends to follow. "We tolerated him since he claimed he had changed from his earlier political position. After all, he worked for the government, didn't he?"

"Working for the government does not absolve one from being a criminal," said the older agent. "Loyal today, traitor tomorrow: the prisons are full of such people".

"Now that you mention it," said Romy, "I think it is curious that he never took even one of us to his house. Simply curious, so much secrecy is not normal now that I come to think of it."

And thus Teddy and Ijigayehu also joined in throwing accusation at their former friend. Dr. Alex wore a serious face as he informed all (specially the two agents) that he had discussed politics at large with none other than the PM ("who can teach all political science PhDs anytime of the day, mind you") and he has zero tolerance for anyone who betrays His trust and becomes corrupt. Not to mention the infamous Red Terror, fumed Dr. Alex who had in the past been heard stating that the victims of that Terror got what they deserved.

The two agents left the Sheraton Six and the luxurious hotel itself after refusing Dr. Alex's invitation to have a drink with the group.

"The dog," exclaimed Romy when the agents had left. "How could he get himself into a 'petrin' and then tell the police we are his friends."

"Have you noticed by the way," said Teddy lighting a new cigarette, "that we do not have in our group anyone from the elite ethnic group?"

"I am from there on my mother's side," Abiyou informed them.

"I thought you said you were from the two big ones," said Ijigayehu.

"Also from there too," said Abiyou. "But my mother is more from the elite group."

"So our group cannot be accused of chauvinism or narrowness", said Teddy with a grin.

"Not at all," said Romy taking him seriously. "What worries me is that they claim they know. What do they really know?"

"But we have nothing to hide, do we?" asked the new member Getty. The others looked at one another.

"In principle we all should and do have a skeleton or two in our closets," said Dr. Alex. Who doesn't, except perhaps the PM? But this is neither here nor there; we are not bad people, no. We have nothing to hide from the State."

They all joined in with a no or a nod of the head.

"I still found the 'we know' statement slightly ominous," persisted Romy. "The agent was looking at us suspiciously as he said it."

"What is there to know?" said Teddy. "We gather here

almost every evening and drink ourselves close to death?"

They did not join his laughter.

"Well we had once discussed the internal problems of the rulers",
said Ijigayehu.

"To support the PM," Dr. Alex pointed out.

"True, but we also talked of some failings," said Jiggy.

"As does the PM himself," said Dr. Alex.

"He can criticize himself and his policies but can we?" asked the new member Getachew.

The group remained silent. Teddy smoked and kept the mocking grin fixed to his face. Dr. Alex and the others drank from their glasses and communed with themselves.

"Maybe my joining you all was not that bright an idea," said Getachew rising. "I should leave you to sort out your problems. I hate to think that I acted as a bad luck for Muktar. Maybe I should stay away."

And with that, Getachew got up and left the group without even paying for the four Jack Daniels doubles he had consumed.

"I told you he would be a problem," complained Dr. Alex. "He will now go around spreading the rumor against us. It could be dangerous."

"You mean..." Romy left it at that but Dr. Alex picked it up.

He said: "Yes, precisely. Never show your wound to a fly. I know them. I left them is what he will start saying as he tries to be accepted by other groups. We must preempt."

"Right away," said Abiyou." He who is not wary gets purged."

Dr. Alex threw him a questioning look and said: "We must inform all and sundry that he wanted to join in much like the desperate flour that befriends the wind but we found him suspicious and pompous and refused."

They all nodded in agreement.

"In fact," went on Dr. Alex, "You Abiyou should start right away since no one will suspect you of ill motives as you are related. Blood has more pull than a magnet."

Abiyou obediently left.

"I do not trust Abiyou will be objective," said Dr. Alex to the others. "Blood is thicker than what he has with us here. We must move on our own to counter Getachew. I will talk to the powerful to forestall any problems or doubts that may come on us because of Muktar. Teddy will handle the waiters here so that they tell the police, if asked, that Muktar was not that tight with us at all. Jiggy, you should also call in your male friends in high places. The most urgent thing is to recruit a new member from the elite ethnic group. Fast. It is protection."

"There is Goitom," said Jiggy. "He is very dumb and boring but he is from there and well connected."

"The desperate marries a pregnant woman" said Dr. Alex, without mentioning the part of the saying that deals with when the child gets born. "He can serve us at least till we get over any possible problems. Remember the hyena limps till it gets to the open field." Dr. Alex was sobering up. He enjoyed such storm in a tea cup moments of crisis during which he acted out like a field commander ordering his group members into action. Doesn't the poor man sit at the Emperor's dining table in his dreams?"

And so, the Sheraton Six now reduced to five agreed to recruit a new dumb member.

That night, after the group had separated, Teddy was in his house when he used his portable phone to call an unlisted member.

"Hello? Who is it?" The hoarse voice was as usual slurred.

"It is me Gidey, Sir" said Teddy using his code name given to him personally by the Minister in charge of the political police to whom he reported directly. "I have something to report. Can I drive over for a drink?"

As Teddy was driving to the Minister's house, Dr. Alex was drunk and asleep in his suite, Jiggy was in bed with a young man she had picked up just outside of the Blue Room,

Abiyou was with Getachew discussing their chances of joining any Sheraton group made up of the elite ethnic group and Roman call me Romy was in her bedroom in her undergarment and in front of her computer, happily surfing the internet searching for photos of nude white men and someone to sex-chat with till dawn.

Epilogue

It was past midnight when Captain Berhanu left his office and entered his Volkswagen to drive back to his home. The City was half asleep, the other half awake and loud in the bars and brothels, in the azmari bets and ill lit kiosks where dangerous but cheap drinks and sex were on the offer.

Here and there he saw police patrolling the streets, armed and in twos, considered by the people as more dangerous than the muggers. Captain Berhanu knew there was crime in the City but he had been angered by one Ethiopian exile who wrote what he claimed was his memoir and falsely claimed he was mugged fifteen times between the Piazza and Arat Kilo. A man staggered out of a bar and started to pee just around the corner. A stray dog shied away from him, suspicious somewhat. As he drove, he saw many people sleeping on both sides of the street and ignored the beckoning stop hand signals being given to him by girls who could have been his daughters if he had had any.

He had had a busy day. He had to drive to Gola Sefer,

Shiro Meda, Entoto and back to Mercato to follow the case of the headless corpse found near the Lideta Sefer. He had few leads and very many suspicions and the people he had interviewed had as usual been reluctant to talk to him openly. Most people were allergic to policemen he knew and was not perturbed. In the distance, he heard a gun shot. And then another. Several dogs barked. A donkey brayed from his right and Captain Berhanu smiled, content that it was not from his left side as it would have been bad luck. He had learnt such things when he was assigned to the rural police posts and he never did scoff at the belief of the people. He knew he had not much that was different to offer, his borrowed science was as flawed as their superstition. His mind went to those intellectuals he pitied who had started to abandon their Christian faith as foreign and resorted to worshiping trees. Others had abandoned their old Coptic faith and adopted a ferenji brand of Christianity that promised them a meeting with Christ every day and exalted weeping and self- loathing. And Captain Berhanu knew that the average Ethiopian had much to cry about with the slightest excuse. As he approached the St. Yohannes Chruch and turned right, he did not make the sign of the cross, did not even look at the church. The street was quiet, the few bars open, with weak street- lights besieged by moths. He recalled the kiosks where warm- hearted prostitutes let young boys like him have sex on credit-- fly now and pay later as they called it subverting an Ethiopian Airlines ad. Such generosity was now long gone, the street girls and whores were more cold hearted, life was much more hard.

Near the Arbegnotch school he saw there were many people sleeping in plastic sheds and cardboard shelters like in Aware, Lideta Mesalemiya, Shiromeda, the sign of the terrible times the City had sunk to. The school itself had the dilapidated look of most buildings, uncared for, neglected, ignored. Ill clad students were now forced a hundred to a tiny room in a three shift school day to listen to underpaid, bored and tired teachers while the children of the rich, like those of the PM, went to the Sanford English School, the French Lycee or other such well kept establishments. If the education system had collapsed the health sector was in even worse shape and Captain Berhanu had to pass several rubbish dumps being scavenged by skinny children and dogs before he reached his home.

As he turned into the dimly lit side street leading to his cold house, he suddenly remembered that he had lived this life for far too many years he cared to remember. He felt as tired and old as the century old City but he also knew that tomorrow he would get out of bed to drive through these same streets to do the same work and to be sensitive to the joy and pain of the City that had been and will continue to be his home.

Nuro kalut mekabir yimokal. If you take it as life the grave can be warm. Like his City.

Printed in the United States
52123LVS00002B/133-207